FREE FALL IN STILETTOS

To Renee
Best Wishes

Love,
Catherine x

FREE FALL IN
STILETTOS

Catherine Louise

Matador
9 Priory Business Park,
Wistow Road, Kibworth Beauchamp,
Leicestershire, LE8 0RX
Tel: 0116 279 2299
Email: books@troubador.co.uk
Web: www.troubador.co.uk/matador
Twitter: @matadorbooks

ISBN 978 1789018 035

British Library Cataloguing in Publication Data.
A catalogue record for this book is available from the British Library.

Printed and bound in Great Britain by 4edge Limited
Typeset in 11pt Adobe Caslon Pro by Troubador Publishing Ltd, Leicester, UK

Matador is an imprint of Troubador Publishing Ltd

Dedicated to all those who believe in me and especially my Mum, who didn't bat an eyelid at the rude bits!

:O *xxx*

CONTENTS

GLAMOUR PUSS FANTASY

January 2002

The kettle hissed as it boiled. I peered out of my kitchen window and gazed at a swirl of smoke escaping a neighbour's chimney pot, which rose then dissipated amidst the blanket of grey clouds looming above; rain looked imminent.

Dirty mugs stacked up by the sink. Stirring my tea, the empty biscuit packet that I'd discarded on the worktop, rather than the bin, reminded me that I'd already eaten the last chocolate digestive. Milk and cereal were the only food left. And unwilling to settle for another takeaway, I was doomed to brave the winter chill and drones of Saturday shoppers. Letting out a sigh, I'd do it later.

Emma, my best friend and flatmate, kept telling me not to get disheartened, in between making me endless cups of tea and filling me up on chocolate biscuits. She always said that cups of tea help solve everything.

A yoyo dieter herself, she'd become a feeder. Secretly, I loved it, even though I kept telling her to cool it with the biscuits. At times, it was hard to resist scoffing a plate of biscuits put under my nose, but no more than four... usually. Except on a bad day when troughing my way through an entire packet was effortless, but only the milk chocolate ones, and just the mini variety you find at corner stores. Things had been depressing lately.

As kids, Emma and I lived down the road from each other. Growing up together, we knew each other's secrets. She had dirt on me and vice versa. She wasn't your stereotypical librarian, usually preferring to chat rather than read books. She said that the chilled-out feeling in the library was calming, and good for her soul, apparently. And that the smell of the library made her want to poo, which we'd both agreed was probably due to her feeling relaxed, more than the smell of books.

Her long, bright and bushy dyed-red hair matched her cherry Doc Marten boots, which she wore without fail; well, mostly. She discovered "vintage" before it was even fashionable, hanging around charity shops spotting great finds. Having invented her own rebellious style, including several piercings, she delighted in lovers discovering her mainly hidden, but large tattoo of a phoenix across her lower back. Sometimes she exposed it wearing a crop top, usually reserved for music festivals. Emma was a natural beauty, just not in the conventional sense.

We both retrospectively shared an appreciation for Madonna in her 1980s phase, each of us owning a pair of long black lacy gloves that we'd discovered in Emma's favourite local charity shop one afternoon, when Emma had dragged me along. We used them for our karaoke and fizzy wine nights in at home, and being short of cash, this was often. Like true fans, we knew all the words to our favourite Madonna songs, *Like a Virgin* and *Into the Groove*, which we regularly murdered. They reminded me of our early teenage years spent at the skating hall roller discos on weekends, wearing baggy trousers, hooded tops and hanging out with boys. They kicked off with the old 80s classics then moved through the era on to stuff like *Pump Up the Jam* and *Dub Be Good to Me*, finishing with up-to-date hits at the time like *Let Me Be Your Fantasy*. A few years later, we swapped the skating for Saturday yoga, but we still clung to the love of music from our youth.

Promising Emma that I'd make progress by myself, reluctantly she'd left for yoga without me. Laboriously, I'd plonked myself back down at the computer, unsure whether I'd keep that earlier promise. Most distractions were welcome, like checking horoscopes and browsing for clothes I couldn't afford.

Clicking the internet icon, I waited for the dial-up connection. It sounded like a Dalek was contacting another robotic machine and waking it from naptime, which always took a stone age before any action occurred on screen. A drowsy tortoise would have been faster. It suited me perfectly.

The lethargy of churning out letters in response to job advertisements (and having built up a stack of rejection letters) had drained my enthusiasm. I wasn't lazy. I just didn't know what I wanted to do. For too long I'd settled in my mundane role in the retail store. The money was poor, and since the rent had gone up a few months ago, I needed to leave. Confirmation arrived with each bank statement landing on my doormat.

I'd been at the same clothing store since starting student life four years ago, gradually increasing the hours. Then reluctantly, after finishing university, I'd unavoidably drifted into full-time employment. That was almost a whole year ago now, and with no ambition to get promoted, moving on was inevitable because the thought of ending up drawing my pension there made me feel like sticking my head in an oven. It wasn't a bad job. Sometimes it was even quite nice. A bit like a comfy cardi, cosy and familiar when you put it on.

Occasionally, I wondered if I'd missed out on life's adventures by not having chosen a gap year. At the time, budget travel, a lack of funds and roughing it in hostels had seemed the off-putting reality, rather than escaping for freedom and adventure. *Champagne taste and beer bottle pockets* – I could hear Emma repeating with amusement after having first heard my mum's expression. She was right.

In a ponderous state, I took some printer paper and picked up Emma's unicorn pen lying beside it, toying with possibilities. She always said her pink magical unicorn pen produced her best ideas, which was ironic being chunky to grasp and almost impossible to write with. Vaguely hoping some magical inspiration might rub off, I began compiling a list. I'd finished it by the time it took for Kylie's *Can't Get You Out of My Head* to play in its entirety.

Playing with the irresistible soft tail dangling from the unicorn's bottom, I twirled it around my finger, reviewing the options. First was chalet girl. Posing around in ski wear with attractive, foreign male instructors. The hot man factor was enticing, but I couldn't ski. Not unless you counted a miserable day I'd once spent at a snowdome in preparation for a week's holiday. And although I baked amazing, mean chocolate brownies, I doubted my cooking skills were sufficient. Next on the list was seeing the Big Apple. But *Camp America* was all I could envisage to get me over the pond. There was zero appeal in having responsibility for annoying kids, along with the accompanying aggravation. Then there was holiday rep. A paid-for holiday in a sunny climate seemed attractive, although entertaining was never really my forte. Lastly, I'd scribbled air hostess.

As a kid, an air hostess ranked in the same league as princess, pop star or model. Any game involving dressing up, being pretty and getting attention. The same concept applied nowadays. Splurging hours over getting dolled up for an occasional night out, with music pumping, accompanied by a glass of pink fizz. Princess rated favourably too, but my fairy tale lacked a prince. Those early fantasies likely inspired my future lust for a uniform.

The closest I'd been to international travel was a ferry to Brittany on a school trip and a brief holiday to Italy (if you could call it that). Both had induced *mal de mer* type scenarios, rather than invoking world exploration. Visiting my grandad on his yacht in Italy sounded glamorous, but the reality had been an ordeal to get there with a car stuffed full of kit, followed by an uncomfortable stay on what can only be described as an overgrown boat, loosely termed a yacht. But it was the Brittany school trip that had left a permanent scar on my memory. Visiting Paris had been the highlight, despite having suffered the embarrassment of a further puking incident on the torturously long coach journey. Someone had told me that a *diabolo menthe* would help ease my queasiness. At the services, I'd naively ordered one in a café, thinking it might help. I'd liked its sophisticated sounding name. But it had tasted disappointingly disgusting, like minty lemonade. Then I'd humiliated myself in front of all my classmates by throwing up and leaving a stench on the coach. But eventually it had been worth it to gawp at the height of the Eiffel Tower and find myself in the French foreign capital. I'd bought a red beret to try and blend in, mistakenly. Well, I was only thirteen at the time.

Circling a ring around air hostess, I felt sure that flying would be different to boat and coach travel. My experiences of working at the student bar and some waitressing had to count as a positive, even if the jobs themselves had been definite negatives, the biggest difference being on an actual aeroplane rather than on *terra firma*.

Picturing myself – a glamour puss, gliding through the air, blue skies on sunny days. Then parading through airports, accompanied by a pilot – preferably a hot one – wearing aviator shades; the glasses were optional.

TROLLEY DOLLY

March 2002

I'd spent two solid hours since 6 am accomplishing *the look*. Putting tremendous effort in to get a no-effort type look (sexy without trying hard). Feeling prepared and minx-like; finally, I was ready.

Wearing my favourite pair of platform stilettos, the shiny red patent ones gave me confidence, even though they made me totter, ever so slightly. They looked good. Emma called them my *filthy, fuck-me heels* to be worn without knickers. When teamed with a short skirt on a night out, slutty or not, they worked fabulously well in bars for getting bought drinks. But an altogether different look was achieved when combining shoes with a suit, giving me an air of finesse, thanks to the versatility of the stilettos. And, I *was* wearing knickers.

Thoroughly inspecting myself in the full-length mirror close-up, a thick layer of make-up stared back. Well-trowelled-on-foundation with a dusting of powder. Black eyeliner made my eyes pop and my lips looked larger than usual, which I'd achieved with perfect precision, colouring in using a lip pencil. I'd meticulously planned my outfit in advance, making sure that it clung to me in all the right places. A long navy pencil skirt with a short matching jacket, skimming my boobs. Nails filed and licked with bright red paint and well-groomed hair tied up in a neat bun. My aim was a modern twist on chic and classy, yet elegant like the airbrushed effect in glossy travel magazines. Satisfied at having accomplished *the look*, I pouted and blew a kiss. I visualised myself joining the ranks of the super-babes and headed out the front door.

♡

'April Budd,' said a loud voice, reeling off my name from a list.

My stomach lurched, and I sprang to my feet. Making my way steadily from the tiled floor in the lobby area of the hotel to the conference room opposite, being careful not to have any mishaps in heels, I was ushered into a room of would-be flight attendants. Stepping onto the low pile carpet, I relaxed my shoulders, feeling relieved at avoiding an embarrassing arse-over-tit topple. Chairs were laid out in rows with a projector screen at the front.

The chit-chat conversation grew noisier as more hopeful candidates filled up the room. Choosing the end of the middle row, I sat quietly checking out the others. They did likewise, coyly glancing at name badges. We'd all obediently pinned them to ourselves, having been instructed by the brisk lady at the door on the way in.

Competition from the immaculately dressed was fierce. Scanning the room, some girls were stunners, with flawless make-up and slim figures. There were only two mature ladies, sat further along my row. The rest, I guessed, averaged early twenties. Towards the back were three exceptionally smart lads, grouped together. Curiously, I wondered if they were gay. They were kind of cute, although not my type and more like handsome contenders for a boy band. The room hushed as someone official started the introduction. Group assessments were next.

Huddled around tables of eight with an assessor hovering, the challenge was to decide the essential items needed on a flight. In the middle of our table was a carton of orange juice, water, a pack of cards, face paint, a pen, a book, toilet roll and biscuits. My stomach rumbled. I quite fancied a nibble of chocolate biscuit. Glancing at my watch, it was only 10.30 amish and still a long way off lunchtime. I had yet to tackle scenario-based discussions, a presentation and interview. I sighed.

Days later, it was no surprise to get knocked back by a polite rejection letter. Privately, I admitted a dismal lack of under-preparation, except for my outfit. Emma held nothing back. She called it piss-poor planning. And she was right. I should have at least eaten breakfast. It might have prevented the can't-be-arsed lethargy that had kicked in, despite the passing placebo effect of a double shot of espresso when I'd been faced with two interviewers. But I let myself off, having read somewhere that you live a far happier life if you're not self-critical. It was easy to forgive myself knowing I had another shot lined up with a Birmingham-based airline. And being closer to home, it suited me better.

Beforehand, I reviewed the list of tips I'd scribbled from memory. I'd learned that being asked *Have you flown before?* meant Have you worked in the industry? *Sim* meant simulator – where the pilots trained, and not the insert for a mobile phone. *Air hostess* was not something I'd naively jabber on about; the correct lingo was *flight attendant, cabin crew, trolley dolly* or *dragon wagon* – for the unlucky ones. Opting out of the voluntary language test was essential. My schoolgirl abilities had previously let me down. Asking about hair and eye colour and what time someone got out of bed in the morning was not enough to be considered basic skills. It left me thinking that a blind date was the only time my limited French would come in handy.

Days later, after the interview, Jet Xpress offered me a cabin crew job by phone, starting in the summer. It was a calm conversation. I politely accepted. Then I replaced the receiver and went hysterical.

A GODDESS IN TRAINING

July 2002

Stuck in traffic and feeling nervous, made worse by needing a wee, I dug my nails into the steering wheel and swore at the cars barely moving ahead.

Finally, pulling up in a car park in the Birmingham suburbs, I got out, loitering briefly to decipher the way in. It looked disappointingly industrial. Pre-fab buildings were dotted about and there was an abandoned, knackered old van in the corner with a flat tyre. Double checking the address, I was in the right place. Faced with what resembled an aircraft hangar, I downgraded my expectations. From the outside, the place didn't mirror my high expectations of a training centre for cabin crew.

Approaching in my direction from down the street, I spotted a very attractive brunette in tortoiseshell sunglasses, wearing a tight-fitting pencil skirt. She was wolf-whistled by a guy in a passing car. I bet she was cabin crew. Looking down at myself, having not been sure of the dress code for training, I'd settled on selecting pleated trousers with kitten heels and a cream coloured, slinky top. Before heading out, I'd given myself the okay in the mirror, but compared to her, I wasn't stylish. My outfit was practical and presentable. Feeling frumpy, I regretted following my mum's advice on what to wear when she'd visited last weekend, which was a *safe* look of casually smart appearance. I'd only asked her opinion as Emma's less-than-conventional dress sense had left me in doubt. Mentally, I kicked myself for having not adopted the sass of my interview apparel. The girl walked straight past me like I was invisible. I possessed neither elegance nor sex appeal. I told myself that I'd consult my wardrobe for style-savvy options tomorrow. The only problem was that other than party dresses and suits (I was accustomed to wearing in-season business style suits in the retail store), I didn't own hot, racy clothes to wear for work. And having almost reached my credit card limit, I doubted it could take the battering required to get my wardrobe up to scratch.

Contemplating that perhaps I was becoming too shallow about looks, I soon shrugged off the thought, *Who isn't at twenty-two?* My redeeming feature was my long blonde hair which usually got me noticed. Fortunately, mum had delivered good genes there. Flicking back my hair, I dashed for the loo.

Entering the training room, I immediately spotted the girl. A vision of beauty. She sat cross-legged, looking lovely and sophisticated. She was gorgeous and completely fanciable – proper girl crush material. She had the smoothest-looking skin and the silkiest, shiny dark hair tumbling elegantly over her shoulders. Her make-up was perfect too. Momentarily taking my eyes off her to look around the room at my fellow trainees, I felt reassured. Not that they were dowdy, but she'd outdone everyone, the only sex kitten amongst us.

'All right chick. I'm Kerrie,' said a deep Brummie accent.

It was the goddess. And she was talking to me. Her voice wasn't befitting of her looks. But grateful for some justice, I instantly liked her.

'Couldn't stand the sun in me eyes over there,' she continued, 'thought I'd come and plonk myself next to you.'

'Hi,' I replied, smiling. 'I'm April, nice to meet you,' I said.

At that moment, a tall, dark and tanned man breezed into the room. He was carrying a large folder which he dumped on the table.

'Good morning. I'm Christian, your trainer, and I'll be taking you through your six-week cabin crew training course,' he said. His eyes scaled each of us in turn.

'Cor! He's a bit of all right candy,' whispered Kerrie, under her breath.

I smiled back. She wasn't the only one to notice.

Intensive Training

The ability to swallow, absorb, digest and fully regurgitate learning proven by passing numerous tests was a skill; along with becoming fluent in airline speak, although I couldn't fathom a reason for replacing words like *collect the rubbish* with *gashing in* and *kitchen* for *galley*.

We were quizzed on trivialities like *Do you push the door or pull it open?* and *Are the additional safety harnesses located top right or bottom left?* and *How many flotation aids are carried on the aircraft?* etc. My level of intimacy with each of the five aircrafts was regularly scrutinised. The emergency drill had been etched in my brain – an itemised list of what to do if it all kicked off – s*hitting* oneself being the reality and the reason flight attendants smelled of perfume – it covered up any *shit* when they breezed by.

Getting our uniform was like being awarded a prize. Pilots got stripes and wings. We got a red lipstick recommendation, heels and hosiery. We had both a summer and winter uniform which was a jacket and two different skirts, which provided a choice. The navy fitted skirt was allowed all year round. I preferred it. The summer skirt was long and floaty with gathered pleats and reminded me of something my gran used to wear. It made me look like a *frumpy dumpy* and I hated it. Apart from on a *feeling fat day*. It skimmed over lumps, bumps and disguised bloating and trapped wind.

August 2002

'Christian, what do we need to wear tomorrow?' Kerrie asked with a huge smile.

He sloped over to her table and perched on the end. I observed him ogling Kerrie. He was a confirmed brunette and boob man.

'Sorry?' he said.

Leaning over, whilst pretending to mishear, he took in a good eyeful of her ample cleavage. Sitting upright, Kerrie encouraged him.

Silly fucking question, I uttered under my breath.

'Good question,' replied Christian whilst raising both his arms and pointing his fingers upwards in the irritating manner I'd become accustomed to. He did it to try and grab the attention of everyone in the room. But it didn't make him any less attractive. 'Listen, ladies; please wear your summer skirts tomorrow ready for the evacuation practice.'

We arrived in Bristol by minibus. It was a purpose-built training ground. The excitable chatter on board had resembled a noisy school outing. When the doors opened,

I'd been pleased to escape. We all tipped out forming a small crowd, ready to be introduced to a real aeroplane. Everyone was dressed as instructed in the obligatory summer skirts, ready to ride the giant slide.

The day before, we'd experienced the simulator for smoke mask training. The headgear had resembled a World War II relic, making each of us look like an extra in a scene from *Alien*. But it had been a good laugh. The only downside was the after-effects of an unavoidable bad hair day – even Kerrie hadn't escaped the dishevelled look.

Inside the hangar there was an aircraft with its huge inflatable yellow slide activated. Not dissimilar to a giant bouncy castle.

'Out of interest, is there anybody in the room that has *never* flown before?' asked Christian.

The echoes of voices in the hangar suddenly hushed as everyone looked around.

'Come on… there's usually one,' he said.

Nobody raised their hand. My heart beat faster. I was damned sure my hands would remain glued to my sides due to the fear of looking ridiculous, having committed to a flying job; although the thought of receiving special treatment from Christian crossed my mind.

'No one. Okay. Good,' he said and continued to explain the exterior aircraft features.

Then we climbed inside. It was a buzz, being in a proper aeroplane for the first time. A frisson of temptation took hold as I eyed up the gadgetry in the cockpit. Having spotted a couple of retro-looking Atari games joysticks, I wanted to press and play. But I kept that urge to myself. We were being watched.

Christian moved on to talk about the *how to* of taking off the emergency door. Knowing that performing this manoeuvre formed part of our assessment (and I didn't want to be the only idiot that did it wrong), I paid attention. Then we each took a turn whilst the engineers fully supervised in case of accidental droppage, causing an expense akin to a mortgage.

'Form a queue, please, ladies and take off your shoes,' said Christian, standing at the front of the aircraft. I bet he was usually accustomed to telling women to take off more than their shoes. I was first in line. Kerrie was behind. 'Now follow me.'

Christian zipped down the slide. I inched forward, peering down at the ground. Christian had positioned himself at the foot of the slide. It looked intimidatingly high from the top, and a long way down to reach the bottom.

'Promise I'll catch you,' Christian called, offering out his hand.

Forced to abandon my fears, I held my breath and jumped. It was a soft landing to start with, not hard like playground slides. But it was faster than I'd anticipated as I whizzed down at speed. My skirt flew in front of my face and acted like a giant parachute. The fabric billowed. There was nothing I could do.

Arriving at Christian's feet in an unladylike heap, I lay there, trying to recover my dignity. He bent over, took my hand and pulled me upright. Then he flashed a smile, whilst I adjusted myself. *Thank God I was wearing clean knickers and not period pants.* (Each month, my *minging knickers*, the ones I kept for that very occasion, made an appearance for a few days before being shoved right back to the furthest crevice of my drawer.)

The other girls followed on behind. A raucous sound of laughter echoed off the walls. Then a few pilots and engineers flocked over. Soon there was a gathering of keen voyeurs to join our party and underwear exhibition. And I didn't care. Christian's motives were perverted. But there wasn't a single girl that didn't queue enthusiastically for another go.

The Captain's Log

September 2002

Stuck to the side of the kettle was Emma's fluorescent Post-it note, which read *Good luck, mate. I got you a present for your 1st day x*. Next to it was a packet of travel sickness tablets. It was partly a joke, but it made me laugh. As a precaution, I swallowed a couple.

It amused me that I was now a fully-fledged flight attendant, even though I'd still never actually flown on an aeroplane before. Most passengers probably had more experience of flying than me. Not that I'd ever share that. But I doubted their heads were as stuffed full of flying facts. Mine was like a saucepan having been left on the boil, bobbing open with streams of bubbles spilling down the sides.

I arrived at the crew room door and paused. Feeling like the new kid at school, I told myself to get a grip. Then taking a breath, I pushed down the handle and walked in. It was vaguely familiar, having visited during training about three weeks ago.

No one seemed to notice me. It was paraphernalia central. Loads of tables and chairs were scattered about. Large cardboard boxes were still lying on the floor, and uniform was still hanging on the clothes rails. The large sofa provided an area to hang out, with a radio for entertainment. It was empty. My first instruction was to find my crew.

Behind me, the door burst open. A pretty, dark-haired girl with a cute dimpled smile made her entrance.

'All right, chick?' she said to me, prompting me to introduce myself as she rifled through her bag without looking up.

'I'm April. Nice to meet you… it's my first day,' I said.

'Ahh, you're one of the newbies,' she said, stopping the scrabbling in her bag to give me the once-over. 'It's a bugger losing your lip gloss.'

I laughed.

'I'm Becky. Don't worry, I'm gonna look after you, chick. We're on the *Dash*. So, any nervous passengers, remember to tell them that if one propeller cuts out then the plane can fly perfectly adequately using the other one.' She smiled, but I knew she meant it. 'Time for the briefing. Come on, I'll introduce you to the flight deck.'

Following the introductions, I became acutely aware of staring at Tom, the first officer. I didn't fancy him. He just looked too young. And they let him fly planes full of passengers with their lives in his hands, and more importantly, mine. At least the captain, called Ron, provided comfort. He looked reassuringly old. He had a large paunch and grey, thinning hair and wrinkles around his eyes. I just hoped he wasn't prone to a heart attack at his stage of life. Our first destination was a short hop to Jersey. As I tried to relax and involuntarily found myself picturing cows, ice cream and lots of old people taking holidays, the crew got up to leave.

I got my first glance of the Dash as it stood on the tarmac, parked on stand... a proper old-fashioned looking propeller aircraft. I'd heard all about it, but hadn't seen it, until now. Disguised in livery, it had been surreptitiously placed amongst its shinier, bigger and much newer contemporary colleagues. It stuck out. It belonged in a museum. It would have been more at home there. It had survived the war effort and escaped retirement. And now, here it was being granted a second life alongside the proper commercial planes. During training, we'd been warned about fearsome flyers being more nervous and suspicious about propeller aircraft. Now, I could see why.

On board, Ron opened the door to the loo, making a loud announcement in his Scottish accent: 'Time for the captain's log. Tom, I want you to record it,' he said whilst locking the door.

Tom looked disgusted. But it made me laugh. As the toilet flushed, Becky waltzed down the aisle spraying a cannister of air freshener. A sea of mist mainly masked the smell as we awaited the arrival of passengers.

Thrilled at having been invited to sit in the flight deck for my first ever flight, I was relieved at Becky's expertise with the jump seat. It pulled out using brute-force from behind the first officer and was a tricky manoeuvre for a first-timer. Becky placed the headset on me and left. Still no one knew it was my first time. I kept quiet and listened to the voices of the pilots going through their checklist.

Then the engines fired up. The sound was louder than I'd expected. A tingle in my tummy turned to a rush of excitement as the aircraft slowly moved. The voices in the headset confirmed that we were on *pushback*. The stench of fumes was strong. It reminded me of travelling on the top deck of a ferry with the wind blowing straight into my face and making me feel ill.

A quick flashback of the Brittany school trip played on my mind. The puke image popped up. The more I tried to banish thoughts of vomit, the harder it became. I didn't have a bag prepared. Tom's well-combed, parted and slicked-back hair was straight in line for receiving projectile spew. Then I remembered the travel sickness tablets that I'd digested earlier and calmed myself. If the absolute worst-case scenario happened, I promised myself I'd resign.

We started to taxi. Waiting for take-off, I firmly held the rim of my seat, hoping for some sort of comfort and protection. In an instant, the sound intensified like a rocket launcher on full blast. Suddenly, hurtling down the runway, my stomach whirled. I fought the thrill of letting out a theme park-style scream. We left the ground and headed steeply upwards, into the clouds, and it was spectacular, being airborne.

Releasing the rigid tension from my arms, my hands were stiff from gripping tightly. It left marks that ate into my palms, like the handles of overloaded shopping bags. And it was awesome – being above the world and seeing it all from the sky.

'Let's go, chick,' said Becky, as she removed my headphones. It startled me. I hadn't realised she was there.

But we had work to do, even though I was too in awe of flying to be bothered.

'We're not full today, which is totally bizarre because these flights are usually always full of pensioners between the ages of eighty and death. We're gonna run down the aisle, chuck everything out and then sit and 'ave a chat. Sound okay, chick?' she asked.

'Err, yep. Let me know what you want me to do,' I said. She laughed and pointed to the back galley.

Heaving the heaviest trolley up the aisle on an ascent in mid-heels was challenging along with balancing tea and coffee pots on top. I did the service whilst she did duty free. Then the seat belt sign went off. A flurry of people attempted to flock to the loos, which was a pain in the ass. Each time someone wanted a wee or worse, it resulted in politely going back and forth with my trolley, timed with toilet entries and exits. Observing Becky, she made passengers wait. I had lots to learn. Service finished, and trollies stowed, we sat on the front crew seats.

'It's a nightmare with toilet disruptions,' I said.

'Yeah. You get used to that, chick. I sometimes get the captain to switch on the seat belt sign when it's impossible,' she said.

'They do that for you?' I asked.

'Yeah. The good ones do. Not the jobsworths, but there's not too many of those,' she replied.

'So, what's next?' I asked.

'Have you seen the bloke with a cock on his head?' she said.

'What?' I laughed, thinking I'd misheard.

'That guy down there; he's gelled up his hair, looks like a cock. What'd you call it?' she asked.

I peeped round the curtain, immediately recognising the offending passenger. Far younger than most on board, he had a Mohican-style haircut, enthusiastically gelled straight up at the front. I sniggered.

'What about nostrils in row 5A? They're coming alive,' she said and put her hand to her nose and wiggled her fingers to demo stray nasal hair. *'Nostril damus.'*

Peeking back through the curtain again, I spotted the big nose in row 5A.

'You're evil,' I laughed.

'Yeah. You've gotta have a laugh, chick. Helps pass the time,' she said. Becky's deceptive, innocent-looking smile suggested that she could get a whole lot worse. 'Your turn.'

'Oh, I don't know. I can't stick my head round again. Looks weird,' I said.

'Here,' said Becky, handing me a black bag. 'You go *gashing in*. I want at least one observation by the time you get back. Think of it as initiation.'

Feeling like a binman, I went through the cabin carrying out rubbish collection duties. I sought anything of comedy value whilst Becky relaxed with her feet up and a magazine – a number one's prerogative. On getting back to the galley, I reported in.

'Comb-over in row 11 and flying low next door,' I said.

'I'll go and look,' she giggled. 'You sort out the trolleys up front and I'll secure the cabin.' She went to do the final passenger checks, leaving me staring at the trolleys, wondering what to do. Moments later she returned. 'You're good. I can't believe you checked out that guy's crotch…

and on your first day,' she laughed as she pinned back the curtain ready for landing.

'I couldn't help noticing when he leaned over to hand me his cup,' I replied, laughing and hoping that the noise from the aircraft muted our conversation to any passengers. Becky had zero concern.

'Didn't think he'd be your type,' she said.

'He's definitely *not*,' I smirked.

'Now, what have you done with my trolleys?' she asked.

'I didn't really know what you meant,' I said.

'Just teasing you, chick. Got new trollies on landing. Soz, mean trick,' she said.

'I set up the tea and coffee,' I said.

'Perfect. Now chill out. You're going to get on just fine, chick. We're having some fun. Better go and take up your seat for landing,' she said.

Creeping back into the cockpit, I didn't know whether to announce my arrival as a casual *hi*, or to keep quiet. Not wishing to distract anyone, I opted for the latter. I tried to be inconspicuous about pulling out the crew seat. But both pilots looked over their shoulder at me, so I casually waved. Then I yanked at the mechanism, caused some noise and pulled the seat into place. I strapped in and relaxed, observing the sunny views. Sandy rock pools were dotted around the coastline.

'Go around,' bellowed the captain. 'Flaps,' he shouted. 'Flaps,' he yelled again. Ron went berserk with a massive *bollocking* aimed at Tom. It felt awkward, being there.

A crash landing flashed through my mind. As we descended, I saw the runway and closed my eyes on coming in to land. It was better if I couldn't see an imminent disaster. And I didn't want to die. Moments later, we smacked down to a jerky journey down the runway with heavy jolting on the brakes pushing me into my seatbelt. And a bit like first-time sex, I breathed a sigh of relief at getting it over with.

Four months later, back on the Dash

Working down at the rear of the aircraft and preparing for a landing in Cork, I felt sick. It was hot. Almost too hot. I rubbed an ice cube over my forehead, thinking perhaps the coolness would ease the nausea. I'd been fine earlier on the last two sectors. I thought the heat was getting to me. The captain bellowed over the tannoy: *Cabin crew seats for landing.*

Earlier, on the way through the airport, I'd had half a chicken wrap. Thoughts of warm chicken now made me want to spew. I held my stomach. As the plane started to descend, the undulating motion felt like a fairground ride after eating too many sweets, and with already feeling ill, the effects seem multiplied. Strapped in, unprepared, too close to landing and with no airsickness bag within grabbing distance, there was nothing I could do. And never having been good under pressure, I had a split second to decide… lap or floor.

Projectile vomit neatly swam in the lap of my skirt. One of the passengers got up and pulled the curtain across. I considered resigning.

In a daze, I found myself being dragged to the loos, stripped and washed. It was *sod's law* I wasn't carrying a spare skirt or my *just-in-case pants*. The pilots decided that they weren't waiting for a replacement crew member. They wanted to go home regardless. Too ill to care, I went along with it. The number one spritzed me with *eau de toilette*. It amplified the pungency of vomit. The plan was to do the demo with my stinking skirt pulled round to the back. The stain was less visible from behind. Never had I felt so ashamed or embarrassed.

INTRODUCTIONS

March 2003

Beginning early on the *Whisper Jet*, with a first sector flight from Glasgow and shuttle runs to Paris, we were due to night-stop in Glasgow. We'd just landed in Paris and awaited a change of flight deck. (Aviation law prevented the pilots working as many hours as flight attendants.)

Timescales of passenger disembarkation and boarding meant frantic preparation. I'd finished checking seat pockets for rubbish (a gross gloves-on-job that involved delving a hand deep into where passengers stuffed nasty surprises) and threw off the gloves to prepare the tea and coffee service, ready for the passenger onslaught or self-loading freight. Almost oblivious to anything else, I felt a gentle tap on my shoulder.

'I don't think we 'ave met,' said an unfamiliar foreign voice. I turned to see a smiling face. 'Marc,' he said as our eyes met, thrusting his hand towards mine.

He looked French, if that were possible, but his accent confirmed it. His appearance seemed to match. His hair looked too long, needing attention, but he had the biggest warm smile, which revealed so many teeth for one mouth.

'Hi, I'm April,' I said, whilst running my hands over

my skirt a couple of times and wiping off the wetness from the ice bucket I'd been adjusting, before accepting his handshake. The double gold stripe across each epaulette showed his first officer rank. I knew the details he needed for his journey log. '98721,' I stated, reeling off my staff number in parrot fashion, just like every other time I'd met a pilot with a clipboard on a flight. He wrote it down.

'Well, it is very nice to meet you, April.' His toothy grin was back on display. 'I guess this is yours,' he said, handing me my black glove that had fallen from the seat where I'd dumped it.

'Thanks,' I replied and smiled back at him, taking the glove. Then I watched him walk back down the cabin. Reaching the entrance to the cockpit, he virtually crawled in, crouching down. I giggled. He didn't need to bow his head, but he was probably used to hitting it on stuff, being so tall.

Later that evening, after landing, we completed the usual duties of looking for leftover property in the overhead lockers, closing down the bars and my not-so-favourite job – seat pocket checks. A blissful thought occurred of kicking off my shoes and landing face first onto a large hotel bed, fully clothed. But obeying the unwritten flying rule, as was dutifully expected by consensus, I'd packed civvy clothes for the bar.

Approaching the bar, I could see Becky, Ron and Jim. I ordered a Malibu and coke and sat quietly with the crew. As I sipped on my drink, the conversation drifted on without me.

At the next table sat the regular prostitute. Unaware as to whether anyone else knew, I'd seen her before. Different night, different punter. There were two men with her tonight. All three were sitting drinking. She held a wine glass, and the two men had pints resting on the table between them. Candidly, I studied her. She was dressed in a short, tight-fitting pastel skirt and jacket. She looked hardened in the face with worn and haggard skin, and the deep lines across her forehead aged her. She wore her straw-coloured hair scraped back, which revealed grey at the roots and looked straggly, even in a ponytail. I couldn't gauge her age but guessed she looked older than she was, possibly late forties. Bruises down her bare legs were evident, even in the dim lighting of the bar.

She parted her legs, pulling her knees apart in an exaggerated manner, revealing that she wore no underwear as she flashed her crotch to the gazes of the men. The film *Basic Instinct* came to mind, although she was no Sharon Stone. As I looked around, everyone else was too absorbed in banter to have noticed. The three of them got up to leave. I wondered whether she kept herself sober or if she needed the drink.

Then Marc arrived. He plonked himself down in the comfy empty seat almost opposite me. Adjusting the angle of his chair, he almost faced me directly from across the table. He sprawled back. I couldn't help studying him, unintentionally. His seemingly thickset body filled the space. He set down two packets of cigarettes, which he balanced on the narrow arm. Having already half smoked the one he'd lit, he threw back his head, confidently puffing out smoke. Cigarette fumes filled the air. I became mildly interested in his smoking abilities, unwittingly paying him more attention. Inhaling the smell, it wasn't unpleasant. It reminded me of being out in a nightclub, even though it was just a bar in Glasgow on a work night. He had a way of authoritatively throwing back his head as he exhaled. Guessing it was an inherent learned trait of being a smoker, I continued watching as he rolled the cigarette around his fingers in a seductive fashion. He was good at smoking – if there was such a thing.

The dark circles around his eyes suggested he needed more sleep, but so did we all. I noticed that when he laughed, it radiated through his face, making his eyes light up and exposing just a few smile wrinkles, but not in a bad way. In an older man type of way, he was attractive. His mannerisms – especially the way he did things with a cigarette in his hands, lips and mouth was sexy. Accidentally, I caught his gaze. Looking across at his face, his eyes fixed directly on me for seconds longer than just a glance.

THE FULL SCOTTISH

Rudely awakened by the harsh and abrupt sound of a mechanical alarm clock, on my mobile I saw it was 5.45 am. I moaned and rolled over. The agitating ringtone needed changing to something more soothing and harmonious-sounding, like a harp. I kept promising myself I'd do it but somehow never did. Reaching for the bedside lamp in the dark, I fumbled for the switch. Trying to recall what I was doing, remembering it was Saturday; Emma would be going to yoga without me again. I lay there, thinking about it.

Yoga had fascinated me since attempting a trial class. Having fallen in love with the idea of trekking off to India one day to learn more and experience the spiritual side of things, I'd signed up for a three-day *get away from it all* convention in Croydon. My dreams were big, but as usual the budget was tight at the time. My now usual class, when I got to attend, was a village hall on the outskirts of Birmingham. And Jessie, a new age hippie, had been my instructor ever since.

It wasn't a natural place of beauty, but it didn't matter. It made me feel de-stressed in the same way as drinking green tea but without the slightly fishy taste – *give me a builder's brew any day.* I also loved how bendy my body was at moulding itself into a pose. And how it felt when I flexed it into a stretch and the release afterwards. It was a feel-good hobby. The yoga trousers made me look great too. The wide band at the top snapped back against my little round bulge in exactly the right place, giving me a perfectly flat tummy. And the tingly feeling all over my body at the end of the session added to my state of relaxedness. Beginning as a yoga virgin, the "three oms" we chanted in class used to make me giggle, but on reaching maturity as a yoga bitch, I'd suddenly got it.

My alarm went off on repeat, disturbing my thoughts and reminding me to get out of bed. I'd allocated half an hour to swing into action, including an extra five minutes to get up. Sprawling out starfish style, I briefly hugged the pillow next to me, feeling not at all like leaving the warmth of a double bed that I had all to myself for another five self-indulgent minutes.

The getting-up routine involved pulling on last night's jeans and top, assembling my hair into some sort of up-do, cleaning my teeth, then making myself smell acceptable before departing for an almighty breakfast. They served an unbeatable *all you can eat* Scottish fry-up. Their breakfast was the best the morning after a thirsty night on the booze. Not that I drank much; it was probably more the dehydrating effects of the hotel air conditioning.

Inspecting my face in the harsh bright light of the bathroom shaving mirror, I peered in to see a magnified and distorted view, providing a revolting close-up of my skin's appearance. All my imperfections were highlighted, and the dark half-moon shapes under my eyes looked a bit slug-like, but there wasn't time for a face mask treatment, not that I could be bothered. As usual, I let myself off by using two fingers, one either side of my lips, pushing them into my cheeks, creating a dimpled happy face and convincing myself it was a passable complexion for an early morning. I'd apply my fake face later – the version I much preferred.

I always checked my appearance in the shaving mirror; it was like getting a worst-case scenario of what I really looked like, in the same way a changing room mirror worked to make me feel grotesque, especially on a big tummy day, accentuating all the wobbly bits I preferred not to notice.

Changing room mirrors were a scam. They made me want to cover up immediately. In shops, I always looked worse than at home. It was all a ploy to make me buy their clothes. But the purpose of looking at ugly me meant that I always knew I looked better than my reflection, because no one saw me that close up – a habit that ironically worked to make me feel good.

I tied my hair into a sort of grunge-style doughnut and left some loose, long blonde strands either side. There were benefits to having long hair in providing camouflage. *That will do*, I told myself, scrunching up my nose at the reflection staring back. Anyway, I'd most likely have the breakfast bar to myself; there were never too many people around at that time of the morning to notice.

Strolling in for breakfast, I was starving. Jim was sat in the corner, scoffing the remainders of what was probably a full Scottish, judging by the empty sauce packets. He waved his knife and gave me a nod. His bloated cheeks obviously contained an overly large mouthful.

Passing by with a casual wave in return, I helped myself from the breakfast bar like a pro and piled up: bacon, sausage, eggs, tomato, mushrooms, a bit of fried bread and toast, all to be washed down nicely with a large mug of English breakfast tea. I walked over to Jim's table with my well-loaded tray.

'Hiyaaa,' said Jim, too full of beans for the crack of dawn. Greedily, he eyed up my plate of food. 'Get it down yer, doll face. Nice one.'

'You're up early,' I said.

He smiled, winked exaggeratedly and skewed his head to one side whilst pointing his knife at me, all at the same time. He always called me *doll face*. I didn't mind. It was Jim. He was an honorary girl. *Doll face* was his pet name for me and any other trolley dolly.

The girls often joked that Jim was afraid to come out. He defended himself against being gay, mainly in the form of a picture of a gorgeous girl he produced from his wallet, conveniently pulling her out when it suited. Everyone had seen it. It was a rare day when Jim didn't refer to being heterosexual.

There were a few gay guys working as cabin crew. The ones that weren't gay would go well out of their way to make sure you knew they were straight. You could usually tell the ones that were gay because often they were better at the job than most of the girls by way of being more attentive to the passengers. Jim didn't altogether fit the gay stereotype. He was more interested in himself than the passengers and was outrageously flirtatious and completely vain – forever checking out his appearance, stroking down his hair and wearing out the mirrors in the toilets. He walked with a quirky bounce to his step, possibly an old dancing habit. He took delight in reminiscing about being a dancer at a nightclub in one of Birmingham city centre's hotspots. I could imagine he was talented on the dance floor. It was in the wiggling of his hips and reminded me of the film *Dirty Dancing* and Patrick Swayze's moves, although it wouldn't be the same sexy with Jim. He was a typical girl in terms of revelling in idle *hostie* gossip and embellishing stories, probably to get attention, which we all knew he lapped up. But still, it was entertaining. He had a way of rolling his eyes and pressing his lips together to show disapproval. And although funny to watch, I'm not sure he even knew he was doing it. He was great to have around for keeping the conversation light and flowing with tales of his previous girlfriends and the latest gossip about the last night-stop, usually involving one of our girls having had a one-night stand with a pilot from another crew. We all loved Jim.

Then Marc showed up. Jim slurped the remainder of his coffee all too quickly, guzzling it in the same way a thirsty dog might finish off a bowl of water before picking its head up and licking itself with its huge tongue. Jim ran the length of his arm across his mouth, wiping up the remnants of breakfast on his sleeve.

'Right, girls; gotta go. Stuff to do, you know. Byeeee.' He nodded at Marc, who was placing his coffee down at my table.

Hell. I looked such a mess. Most crew had breakfast in their room. *Why didn't he?* Appearing without the aid of make-up was made worse when Marc sat down in Jim's spot, directly opposite, with an unobstructed view of me naked in the face. Nothing against Mother Nature, but I preferred to buy my beauty in products, and happily slapped it on to enhance my assets and cover up the ugly bits. I hadn't minded Jim seeing me in my raw state; he didn't count. A close-up inspection was not something I'd prepared for. Resigning myself to being caught out on this occasion, that mistake wouldn't happen again. Casually, I pulled a few more strands of hair down each side of my face, attempting to conceal a bit more; not that it worked, but it made me feel better.

I'd hoped Jim would stay, just a bit longer. He could have detracted from my lack of make-up. And sparked a conversation, so I didn't have to make the effort of friendly banter with a foreign man I hardly knew, and at such an ungodly hour. No such luck. It was bad enough having to try with passengers; at least I was paid for that. Chowing down on a greedy breakfast had been my plan. But now the massive plateful that lay in front of me made me feel self-conscious. I poked my fork at it then stabbed a sausage.

Marc rested his elbow on the seatback of the chair next to him. I couldn't work out if he was self-assured, like the way he smoked his cigarette, or just very chilled out. Maybe it was a continental thing. He looked casual and at ease, wearing a baggy grey and black stripy top.

After taking a swig of coffee, he fixed his eyes on me. I could feel them even as I averted my eyes down to my plate. When I glanced upwards, his large teeth were so noticeable and on full display, accompanied by his huge grin. I couldn't help checking them out. They seemed in good order. Now I understood what people meant when they talked about horsey mouths. As he smiled, his eyes seemed to shrink by comparison. Then I gazed back down at my breakfast for fear of staring. He put down his coffee cup and ran his fingers through his tousled dark hair before resting his other arm back on the table and picking up his cup again.

Maybe he'd start the conversation soon as he'd invited himself to join me at my table, and without asking me first. But even if he'd asked, I would have been obliged to say *yes* and if he'd have sat somewhere else, then I'd have been obliged to ask him over. So, I suppose it was irrelevant. He would have ended up sat there anyway. Forced to put on my smile, the one I used for passengers, I thought I'd ask him about Paris.

'Nice guy, Jim,' Marc said as he sipped at the dark, strong-looking coffee which resembled diluted tar. Seeing him drink it, I was confident of him being fully alert to fly an aeroplane, in much the same way a poker up his backside would have had a similar sobering effect.

Pleased that he'd taken the initiative, I replied, 'Yeah, he's a lively character all right.'

'What is that you're eating?' Marc pointed at the toast I was eagerly devouring, piece by piece in manageable mouthfuls and in quick time to get out of there fast.

'Marmite on toast. Haven't you ever tried it?' I asked.

Obviously, he hadn't, or he'd have recognised the smooth brown goo. He eyed it up, with a kind of fascination.

'No. It looks 'orrible,' he said.

I laughed and tore off a small triangular segment. 'Here. Try a bit. You'll like it.'

He held it between his fingers, looking at it briefly, then he sniffed it. The corners of his mouth turned down.

'Doesn't smell like you're supposed to eat it,' he said.

'Well, that coffee doesn't look like you're supposed to drink it,' I retorted. 'Actually, Marmite is very good for you, full of vitamins and delicious. Go on, just try it – you never know; you might really like it.'

Sometimes I could be so evil. I'd just impressed myself at how innocent a suggestion it had sounded. Trying not to laugh, I just watched and waited. Reluctantly, he bit on a corner. After a couple of chews, he resembled a small child having just tried blue cheese for the first time.

'Tastes disgusting. 'Ow can you eat that stuff?' he asked. I wasn't sure if he was more appalled at me for eating it, or whether his horrific facial expression was due to the taste alone. Reaching for a napkin, he spat out the contents then swigged down the rest of his coffee, which was sure to extinguish any remaining tastebuds.

'Well, you either love it or you hate it.' I couldn't stop myself laughing, and I tried desperately to prevent the chewed contents of my mouth from spraying the table. Marc's face was still screwed up, which was all the funnier. Eventually, I managed to get some words out. 'So, where's your breakfast this morning? Aren't you hungry?'

'Not after that,' he said, looking at my toast and only half smiling. 'I'll stick with this.' He raised his cup. 'Excuse me whilst I get another.'

He probably went off to scrape his tongue clean, somewhere I couldn't see him. I wolfed down as much of my plate as I could, not wanting to scoff the lot whilst he just observed and drank coffee.

It was okay to eat food with someone else if they were eating too, but not with someone watching and definitely *not* with a stranger or almost stranger. It was a self-conscious thing, protecting me from a fear of embarrassment, like getting it round my face and not even being aware that I had egg or tomato sauce dripping around the corners of my mouth and some sort of sausage grit stuck between my teeth when smiling. If they were eating too, it made them equally as exposed to the vulnerabilities. Maybe I was far too vain.

Dabbing the napkin around my mouth, I then rubbed my teeth with my finger to guarantee no disgusting ugly tooth incident. A quick flick of the tongue, and all was good. When Marc returned, he had another hardcore full-strength coffee. We chatted about working and past naff jobs.

'Come on, you can't compare wrapping chicken in a factory with a load of ex-criminals, to mopping out toilets in a nightclub,' he said, shrugging his shoulders, waiting for my reply.

'If I told you what went on in those toilets and what I mopped up, then believe me, it's far worse than handling fists full of chicken. I'm eating breakfast, so I won't give any more details other than to say that ladies' toilets are far worse than men's. Men's just smell the worst.'

I was certain I had one-upmanship on the worst jobs scoresheet. Then thinking about how I'd just dragged the conversation down to a level of discussing toilets, I sat and sipped my tea without saying another word. When

I'd almost drained the mug, I left the last swig to enjoy like a chaser following the final mouthful of food. Then I knocked it back and held on to the mug, enjoying the soothing warmth on my hands.

'What about the future? What job do you see yourself doing in the future?' he asked.

'I like the airlines. Perhaps long haul. See some places. Travel the world and get paid for doing it,' I laughed.

'Why not? I am always on the lookout too. I want to make captain.'

'I'm sure you will, when you're old and wrinkly enough,' I joked. Then I glanced at my watch. 'Well, I think I'd better go and make myself decent now,' I said, resting my mug down on the table.

'You don't 'ave to go yet; you've still got time,' he said, whilst holding up his wrist and flashing his chunky wristwatch.

'You don't have make-up and hair to worry about, so that's why you still have time,' I replied, getting up to leave.

' 'Old on; let me 'elp you,' he said. I had no idea what he meant. He reached out with my napkin and gently held my face with one hand as he dabbed my cheek with the other. I could feel myself blushing. 'A bit of sauce, I think.'

I don't know how long I stood there staring, but I managed to blurt out, 'See you later,' before darting out of there. *Damn, how could I have been so careless to have left sauce over my cheek?* Next time, I'd check my whole face and not just my teeth.

Back in my room, I thought more about the sauce incident. I'd fled when he touched me. A bit uncool. But I wasn't trying to impress him. I didn't think I was. No one had ever wiped my face before apart from my mum, when I was a kid, obviously.

I threw on my uniform, all except for the tights, which called for careful handling to avoid ladders. Almost everyone complained about the uniform, but I liked it. The navy-blue colour suited me, and the skirt highlighted my waist and hips, revealing a pleasing silhouette, like the 1960s fashion icon Brigitte Bardot, or so I thought. When the jacket was buttoned, it pulled in just enough to accentuate my waist. The blouse was a pale sky blue. We wore a patterned scarf, with contrasting flecks of white, which wrapped around and draped across one shoulder. The tights were tan coloured, just dark enough that if you'd forgotten to give your legs the once-over with a razor, you could just about get away with it. But I'd never tested out that theory for more than a couple of days and then only if I'd been in too much of a rush. The shoes gave me a bit of height, making me almost five foot eight. It was all finished off with a daring dash of deep red lipstick, called *red light*, the type of colour I wore as a teenager to tart myself up during the red lipstick and high heels brigade phase in sixth form. Somehow, the lipstick suited the navy colour, and without it my face looked washed out. It also drew out my blue eyes. I loved my *tarting* stick and applied it with gusto along with a good liner so as not to get *trout pout* – where the lipstick sort of runs and makes me look dodgy, like I've applied it on a bumpy car journey. A dusting of powder completed the look. Then I tackled my hair and tied it into a neat bun, finished off with a light spritzing of spray to hold it in place. I rubbed *Anni Sui* perfume over my wrists and neck and then created a high

42

up misty cloud of droplets to walk through just to perfect the overall finish, as was my routine. A heavy perfume was too much, I had learned. It made you smell like an overenthusiastic duty-free shopper, but an *eau de toilette* worked just long enough over the course of a day to linger nicely and cost less too. Good old toilet water. Picking up tips as I went along, looking polished was the game; the epitome of sexy sophistication was my aim. I got the whole art down to about thirty minutes, which wasn't bad. Tossing the remainder of stuff that lay about my room into my wheelie case, I was good to go. I say *tossing*, but it was a well-thought-out method and logical manner that I could implement fast. It involved stuffing all available extra orifices, like shoes, to provide extra room.

I headed to the foyer to meet the crew. Marc was sat reading a paper. I wondered if he'd since thought about wiping my face. He'd probably wiped loads of girls' faces. He was French after all, I reminded myself. *Didn't the French dry hump their mates from a playground age?* The napkin thing was probably nothing.

We were all flying back to Birmingham (positioning) for an airport standby. We strolled over the road to the airport, wheeling our cabin bags. All of us attempted to keep a low profile in the airport lounge until boarding time.

'Looks like we're sitting next to each other,' Marc said, as he reached down to pick up his pilot briefcase. 'We can finish our earlier conversation.' I wasn't aware that we hadn't finished *our earlier conversation* as he'd put it, so I just smiled. 'Sorry, I just 'ave some administration which I 'ave to catch up on too,' he added.

Good, I thought. I wouldn't wholly ignore him, but his paperwork was a valid reason not to have to chat the whole time. He told me about his degree in something properly intelligent sounding like aeronautical physics, which to me meant a degree in becoming a pilot, and I'm sure he mentioned maths at some point too. More concerned with what I was going to be wearing to a girls' night out at the pub that evening with Emma, and mentally planning my outfit, I vaguely listened. Until I felt my tights catch on the Velcro patch inconveniently tucked underneath the seat edge, then I stopped listening altogether.

Like a boobytrap, a continual strip of Velcro ran along the underside edge of the seat, holding a lifejacket in place. Industrial-strength tights would have been the only resistance against getting caught out. If I happened to tuck my stocking-clad legs close, I was guaranteed a ladder and mistakenly I did it every single time. At no point were anyone's legs safe clad in anything less than 20 deniers. Fortunately, I wasn't a passenger (positioning) too often, or it would have bankrupted me. The grooming allowance we were given wasn't exactly compensation. Bulk buying in packs of five for £2.79 was the best bargain I ever found.

'Oh, bugger it,' I said.

'What is wrong?' Marc said, looking up and putting down his pen.

'Just caught my tights on that bloody Velcro strip. I'm always doing that.' I rubbed my fingers across the bumpy patch and the couple of holes it left after pulling free.

Marc shifted his papers to one side and peered down at my legs. 'Still look good to me,' he said with a cheeky grin.

'Well, maybe you could help and get my bag down from the locker whilst I whip these off for the replacement ones in my case,' I said seriously.

'Sure,' he replied, detecting my sense of humour loss.

Marc's eyes bulged. Obediently, he got up to bring down my case from the locker.

'Don't look,' I said.

He diverted his eyes. Wriggling in my seat, I was able to slip off my shoes, raise my thighs and part push down my tights by inserting my hand down through the waist of my skirt. Then I shimmied the tights down and in one swoop pulled them to my ankles. It was a similar procedure in reverse to replace them with a new pair.

Tights were the bane of my life as cabin crew. If I managed to get through a day without laddering a pair, then typically I'd have holes in the toes from all the running around. The holes became big toe *manglers* and were so painful after a day on my feet. Anticipating the heavenly relief of freeing my toes made me rush to my car to tear open the tights, relieving my fat red toes from being pinched at having burst through. On hot days, the issue was amplified from sweaty toe swelling. Standby days were also bad news. Being called out on standby meant literally jumping into action. Putting on a pair of tights at speed was an impossibility, especially with long nails. Preservation of tights meant spending standby days dressed in them ready to go, just in case. The only benefit to wearing tights was the elasticated band at the top that pulled in my stomach like free liposuction when I'd gorged myself on too much crap / crew food – unidentifiable morsels in a hot silver packet with a cardboard lid.

Having arrived back in Birmingham, I took up residence on the leather sofa in the crew room.

'What d'yu reckon? Is it my size?' Jim poked his head through the clothes rails and had taken the opportunity to put on a blouse and skirt then started happily parading around in front of us in his socks. The radio was playing, and he was shaking his arse to *It's Raining Men* and generally being outrageously camp and funny.

'You're such a fool,' Becky said. 'Anyone could walk in.'

He didn't care. I offered some encouragement. 'Here, let me help you finish the look.' I offered him my lipstick, which he couldn't resist. Tying one of the scarves around his neck, he was all too pleased. He mimicked a trolley dolly walk and pose, before turning up the radio and going for it disco style, like an over-indulged child on Haribos.

'Well, I 'ave to go back to Paris now. Nice chatting to you,' Marc said with a raised voice over the sound of the radio as he stood over me. I was lying back on the sofa with my shoes kicked off, using a box as a footstool to rest my feet. Too comfortable to bother moving but also trying to act nonchalantly, brushing off the sauce incident, I didn't move.

'Have a good trip,' I said, pretending to be distracted and raised one arm to give him a wave. The other was holding my mobile ready to text Emma about putting the fizzy wine in the fridge. Marc was just about to exit the room, having grabbed the door handle, when Jim rushed up to him from behind and gave him a whacking great slap on the arse. Instinctively, I drew a sharp breath in disbelief and cupped my face with my hands. You could tell it would have smarted. Jim stood still waiting for a reaction, possibly realising he'd overdone it. It could have gone either way. Marc turned around, gave him a harsh stare, then raised his middle finger before heading off. He was amazingly self-controlled.

As the door closed, we all burst out laughing. Jim had felt the fear. He'd already stripped off his dressing-up clothes in record time.

'Ouch,' Becky said. 'You went too far that time.'

'Nah. He loved the attention. Anyway, just us girls now that your boyfriend's gone,' Jim said, trying to tease me.

'What?' I said, looking over my shoulder to catch an eyeful of too much bare flesh. Jim stood in his boxers, hastily trying to get his trousers back on.

'Yeah. I noticed he was a bit friendly with you, chick,' Becky said. '*Clearly* Marc came over to say bye to *you*, not us.'

Getting up to check through the box of roster changes, I thought about Marc. He was kind of cute for a French guy, even if he wasn't on my current hot list scale along with Brad Pitt.

The phone rang. It was crewing. We all held our breath. Becky delivered the news that it wasn't a call of duty. We were free to go.

THE MOTHER OF ALL ROSTER CHANGES

Crewing were nobody's best friend. They determined your roster, and like the ultimate rulers – we obeyed. They also controlled the jinx factor – roster changes that turned plans to mush. It affected us all – getting screwed over with changes and forcing a reschedule of any social life. No one was immune. Crewing was a dirty word. An *us* and *them* scenario.

Everyone hated doing Paris. The passengers were often difficult or rude, sometimes both. Those with armfuls of hand luggage provided a challenge, having raided duty free prior to boarding. Attempts to drag on oversized bags were a common occurrence. The situation was exasperated by telling passengers that their bag might fit into the overhead locker if they pushed hard enough. Slamming lockers shut was a regular irritation. Maybe because the flights were usually full, I noticed the annoyances more. But I didn't flinch if a passenger was obnoxious. I'd developed a protective bubble. Attempts to burst it occasionally occurred with the exceptional moron.

If a crew member was really pissed off, then the removal of bags for the hold easily infuriated some. Small things provided job satisfaction.

Paris Charles de Gaulle Airport (CDG) intimidated me – not something I liked to admit, being a professional flight attendant. But it was one of the largest airports in the world. Trying to decipher my way around, dressed in uniform, felt like I should have known what the hell I was doing. Ironically, I rarely did. People approached with questions, not realising I lacked basic navigation skills.

Crew rooms were sometimes a devil to find. The Parisian room was no exception. The safety of my home base was always preferential. Contending with getting lost and experiencing a language barrier, all whilst under a time constraint, was stressful. Tiredness could amplify a bad situation, and sleep deprivation was an everyday normality, but at the wrong time of month, my capabilities lapsed, and it took some restraint not to sit on my wheelie case and cry.

June 2003

Thumbing through the roster change files, I spotted my name on paper and automatically I let out a tut. On closer inspection, it was bad ass – first involving a positioning flight to Paris. Then operating four sectors followed by a night-stop in Paris. *The jinx factor*, I mumbled to myself as my shoulders slumped. There was only one potential upside. The remote possibility of seeing Marc. But it wasn't likely. Any pilot could have been tasked with working out of Paris.

It should have been an easy day with shuttle runs to Dublin. But it was too late to sack it off, swap the duty or even go sick. Putting my CDG fears to one side, I reluctantly put on my fluorescent vest to go airside. Locating someone available in the air car shed – *a bit like a man cave where mainly men playing on walkie-talkies hung out* – I was taken directly to the aircraft. That action averted the first potential trauma of finding the right aircraft. Several were parked up on stand.

'We're delayed,' said a whispering voice from an unfamiliar crew member as I entered the cabin. The passengers had already boarded.

'Thanks for letting me know,' I replied.

It was no surprise – an epic day being made even longer with a further delay. The captain announced that we'd missed our air traffic control slot. Code for a very long boring wait ahead. It didn't really matter to me. My plans for the evening had already turned to dust. It reminded me to text Emma to cancel our night at the pub, again. I wasn't reliable anymore. She'd probably be expecting it. And as she used to say, it let her know that although I hadn't been seen in a while, I wasn't lying in a ditch somewhere, undiscovered, which was another saying she occasionally repeated after hearing my mum say it.

Feeling conspicuous in my uniform, I located my seat. The mature lady next to me glanced my way, probably eager to ask when we'd take off. We politely smiled and nodded at each other and thankfully she didn't ask.

The regular sound of the call bell indicated the rising level of passenger intolerance. The operating crew members were doing well fending off irritable passengers, mostly getting grief about connecting flights. The only places to escape were the galley – behind the tiny curtain – or the loos. I opted for the galley every time. Someone always wanted the loo.

We began pushback one hour later. I was trying to work out the difference in time between *zulu (z) time* and the local time in Paris, but I had developed a cloud of brain fog, making me totally incapable of a simple calculation. Staring at my schedule, I tried to clear the haze from my brain, but it refused. The pilots often wore two watches for travelling across time zones, which suddenly made perfect sense. The effects of sleep deprivation and shift work meant that simple tasks became complex. *Were they one hour ahead or did I need to add two because it was summer time?* The harder I tried, the less sense it made. I looked at my roster again, then kicked myself having noticed the indication that I'd be staying put on the plane the other end.

Later than scheduled, we arrived in Paris. I checked my appearance in my compact mirror and reapplied a layer of lipstick. Feeling lethargic from seat syndrome (too long spent sitting in a seat), my bum had numbed. As I heard footsteps approaching, I mentally prepared to jump-start into action.

'Aha. We meet again.'

I looked up to see Marc loading his bag into the overhead locker at the front of the plane, a few seats away from me. Instantly, a smile crept over my face.

'Hi, Marc,' I said.

' 'Ello. 'Ow's it going, April?'

He finished stuffing his bag into the locker, turned to face me and stood smiling, with his hands on his hips.

'Good, thanks. Eaten any Marmite lately?' I asked.

'Oh, you remember that?' he said, nodding his head and grinning. 'It tasted like dried blood.' We both laughed.

The way he pronounced *blood* sounded more like *bluurrrd*. Hearing his adorable accent, it didn't matter that conversation-wise we were on vampire territory. I could listen to him telling me anything – an instructional airline manual would have sounded sexy read aloud by him.

Moments later, Jim boarded, followed by Henri.

'Hey up, doll face,' said Jim, holding up his hand for a high five.

'Jim,' I said, high fiving him back.

'What are *you* doing here?' I asked.

'Same as you,' he said.

As I approached Jim for a hug, he put up a stop hand, lollipop lady style, then began spritzing with aftershave and dowsing himself in a cloud of deodorant, leaving a visible lingering mist of vapour and a stench of man throughout the cabin. Then he grabbed me for a hug, after which he stood back and patted down his hair.

Marc popped his head out of the cockpit. He took a breath, then coughed. I'm sure he was about to say something. But instead, his mouth turned up at the edges, and grimacing, he wafted away the pungent odour of Jim's body sprays before he withdrew back into the cockpit.

'I've had frogs the last two days,' Jim said, rolling his eyes.

'Well, you've more of that to come,' I said.

Jim went on a verbal tirade of *fucking* this and that, interspersed with *crewing* and *bastards* thrown in now and again. It alluded to a clear picture of having been screwed over with a roster change too. Jim had already been in

Paris for a couple of nights, confirming my suspicion that they were short-staffed.

Meanwhile, I observed that Henri had already started checking seat pockets. I shouted down the plane, 'Hi, Henri, I'm on it from the front.'

'Nice to see you, April,' he shouted back in a heavy French accent that almost rolled his words into one.

I had to listen carefully, or just politely nod, when I didn't want to ask consecutively for him to repeat everything. But he didn't mind. He was nice. He'd looked after me in Toulouse when I'd worked away from base for a week. He'd showed me around and we'd had a mini shopping spree together. Henri was also very good-looking and although *I* didn't fancy him, I could see his appeal. His afro hair was always slicked back, Michael Jackson style but without a ponytail. He wore glasses with big black rims and had this funny mannerism of adjusting them between his finger and thumb as he talked. They were probably a fashion statement. Not everyone could get away with his style.

Grabbing my bag from the overhead locker and speedily applying a layer of gloss over the red lipstick, I smartened myself up like a pro, ready for the self-loading freight. My day had dramatically brightened. I felt pleased. Jim and Henri were awesome crew. Parisian passengers could throw us any curveball. And Marc was a big bonus. I hoped we'd have drinks later.

Jim approached the back galley. He came right up to my nose and gave me a weird stare.

'A bit overenthusiastic with the lippy, doll face. Check yourself out in the mirror,' he said, tapping his teeth.

'Oh God,' I said as I darted into the loo for a close-up mirror inspection. Red lipstick was all over my two front teeth, like I'd let a kid loose with a crayon.

It wasn't the first time. It was a hazard of rushed lipstick application applied too deep on my top lip. The excess was removed fast, using a finger and squeaky toothbrush action. I hoped that Marc hadn't witnessed my Dracula smile.

After completing the first sector and with most passengers having departed, we were left with those requiring special assistance. Amongst them was a little old lady travelling alone. As she waited for her wheelchair, I kept her company.

'Is it good to be home?' I asked, attempting polite chit-chat.

'Oh no, dear,' she said. 'I live in Paris. Every now and again, I visit my daughter over here in Birmingham. She doesn't like flying, you see.'

'How did you end up living in Paris?' I asked.

'That's a long story,' she said.

'So, you must speak great French?' I asked.

'Of course. After all these years, I'm fluent, dear,' she said.

'I would love to learn French properly,' I replied.

She beckoned me closer and whispered into my ear. 'If you want to learn French then sleep with a Frenchman.' She tapped her nose, gave me a wink and a naughty smile.

Stumped for a reply, my mouth possibly gaped open. I wasn't sure. She had to be in her eighties. An unwelcome image of an older couple having sex flashed through my mind. But she looked such a sweet old granny, a bit *Miss Marple-esque* wearing a brown coat and crocheted hat, even though it was summer. She looked well past the age of remembering sex, let alone having any interest in it. I thought about my gran. She wouldn't have handled the shock, never mind the advice.

As the wheelchair assistance arrived, I accompanied the lady to the front of the aircraft. Intrigued by her revelation, I whispered into her ear, 'You fell in love.'

'That's the secret, my dear,' she replied.

That story I wanted to hear. I imagined a romantic war tale scenario. As she was lifted off, I waved her goodbye. She made me smile.

A banging noise diverted my attention to the back of the aircraft. I looked around. All the crew were busy gossiping in the front galley. The toilet sign was illuminated, meaning the door was engaged. But I'd previously locked it, storing the gash bag inside before landing. When I checked, the gash bag had been moved outside. Then I heard a whimpering sound. I put my ear close to the loo door and listened.

'Come on, you've got to hurry up,' came a man's voice from the cubicle.

I wondered if it was my first encounter at meeting a randy twosome who'd badly timed an attempt to join the mile high club.

'Right, that's it. Pull your pants up,' continued the man's voice.

There was barely room for one person to manoeuvre. And they weren't the nicest cubicles. Not that toilets are *nice* places, but some are worse than others – like chemical toilets at festivals. I'd first been introduced by Emma at an event. And aeroplane toilets were almost on a par – an incubator of smelly filth that nobody wanted around their private bits. If the smell alone wasn't off-putting enough, then there was huge potential to bash and bruise delicate parts on stuff like the soap lever. I imagined how it might work, planning moves for two. It wasn't romantic.

I stood aside and waited. I'd developed a *nothing would surprise me* attitude at having experienced the worst and best of working with the general public. The worst was being handed a sick bag with the contents dribbling down the side.

Then a man came out of the cubicle holding the hand of a toddler-aged child. I put on my flight attendant smile and wished them a pleasant onward journey.

THE PARIS NIGHT-STOP

Knackered and ready to drop, it was 10.15 pm French local time and 9.15 pm by my watch. All five of us, including the French captain (whom I didn't know), Marc, Jim, Henri and I, piled into the air-car which took us back to the terminal. There were various things to drop off at the crew room before finishing for the night.

The Paris crew room was much smaller than I was used to in Birmingham. It was poky. Five of us filled it. There'd been a rumour circulating about the company closing it down, to save costs. I doubted it. Based on size alone, I couldn't see how they were going to make much of a saving by transferring staff.

Marc sat down at a table, not appearing to do anything. Jim and I hung around, awkwardly. Henri (who was the number one on the flight and in charge) fiddled with paperwork, whilst finishing whatever it was he had to do.

A conversation started about getting to the hotel. There was no taxi booked, which meant contacting the airline. The French captain announced that he was making his own way home and promptly scarpered. Henri offered Jim a lift and that didn't extend to inviting me – his excuse being that his car was quite small, and space was limited with all the stuff he was carrying. He told me that I was better off getting a lift with Marc. Instinctively, I turned to face Marc to gauge his reaction. Aware I'd been stitched up, I felt my face flush.

'Of course, you should come with me. I'm going to the 'otel for a drink in the bar anyway,' Marc said. Immediately, he got up and produced his car keys from his pocket.

'Thank you,' I replied.

I was partly relieved; I didn't want to be stranded in Paris trying to negotiate a ride back to the hotel via the airline, or worse, a crew bus and a taxi. And partly I was pleased that Marc was going to drive me there.

'I'll meet you outside the crew room door in five minutes if that's okay?' I said.

'Sure. No problem,' replied Marc.

The prospect of travelling in Marc's car meant a quick trip to the loo was necessary to spritz with deodorant and perfume, digest a handful of mints and to check and remove any possible dodgy lipstick / tooth incident. (I always kept mints in my bag to avoid dog breath or in extreme cases smelling of *one thousand yaks* – either me or someone else.)

Marc was waiting for me outside the crew room. He picked up his bag when I approached, and we strolled back through the airport towards the car park. As we walked together, he removed his tie, then his epaulettes.

'Why you doing that?' I asked, pointing to his epaulettes.

'I don't like people to know I'm a pilot,' he said.

'Why not?' I asked.

'It's a bit different being a pilot in France than it is in the UK. Firstly, I don't want to draw attention to myself. Also, people don't speak to you if they know you're a pilot 'ere. Or worse, they'll try and take advantage. In France, being a pilot is per'aps more respected than being a doctor or lawyer even. It's crazy like that 'ere,' he said. Loads of pilots I'd seen loved to show off. It seemed that he wasn't one of those. 'I once went to a party dressed in jeans and a t-shirt and everyone else was dressed in suits. Business people and top earners, that kind of thing… and I mean everyone. I really stood out. No one talked to me because I didn't fit in. But I'm not gonna get dressed in a suit to get drunk. I didn't tell anyone I was a pilot, but somebody found out, and people's attitudes changed towards me. It was so false.'

It didn't sound like much of a party to me. *Who gets dressed up in a suit to go to a party?* Privately, I questioned whether he was either moody or had a stubborn streak. Perhaps both. But feeling the tiredness catch up with me, I just listened.

Allowing my mind to wander, I pictured a scene from *Pride and Prejudice*, where Mr Darcy strips off his well-fitting jodhpurs and riding boots by the lake. There wasn't a logical connection between Marc and Mr Darcy other than the getting undressed and stubbornness aspects. It prompted a distant memory of the only Darcy quote I could recall from sixth form days: *haughty, reserved and fastidious*. Marc's stubbornness made him *Darcy-esque*, minus the jodhpurs, horse and riding whip, although I bet he'd look pleasing on the eye.

A curiosity made me slow my pace, holding back about a step behind Marc and fixing my eyes on his rump.

His trousers skimmed over his shapely pert arse, which came to an abrupt halt as we arrived at the lift. He pressed the button.

'I'm on basement level,' he said.

Obscuring my view as he turned to me, the sound of his voice brought me back to the real world. *How long had I been quietly staring at him? Did he know I'd been checking out his bum and the way he walked?* My face flushed. The doors opened.

'There's my car,' he said.

A black Audi TT was parked straight ahead. Whilst Marc paused to fiddle for his keys in his pocket, I went and stood by it, resting my trolley case upright.

'You know, you give away your profession by the car you drive,' I said.

'You got the wrong car!' he grinned.

He pointed to his. Next to the shiny Audi TT was an old French Renault, which highlighted the dents and its aged appearance. It could have passed for the worst clapped-out banger in the car park, with ease.

'My good one's at 'ome. I just use this as my runaround,' he said, smiling at me.

I picked up my case, shuffling over to his car.

'We drive on the right in France,' he announced. Then he grinned some more and opened the passenger door for me, finding it all very amusing. Then before I'd even grabbed the handle on my case to walk round to his side, he quickly slammed shut the car door.

''Old on; just a sec,' he said.

He reopened it and dipped his head inside whilst I stood back and waited. His car must have been a tip. It took longer than just shifting a few items off the front seat.

'Mine's a whole lot worse,' I lied, unsure whether he heard and feeling a bit guilty because he was doing me an unexpected favour.

My car had not long come out of the garage and had been courtesy valeted as part of the service. It never looked good otherwise. Usually, it operated as a permanent bin on the passenger side. We had that in common, it seemed.

'Give me a minute,' he said, poking his head out over the car roof.

'Okay,' I smiled back. It must have been completely filthy. It took him ages.

'Okay,' he announced, holding open the door for me and gesturing with a grand sweeping arm movement. I wondered where he'd shoved the rubbish.

'Is it weird, sitting on the right without 'aving a steering wheel?' he asked.

In an air guitar fashion, I took hold of my steering wheel and mimicked driving.

'I drive to the airport and back in my sleep, probably wouldn't notice if it was left or right,' I giggled. He laughed. Mentally, he ticked a check box.

We chatted about work on the journey. It only took a handful of minutes to arrive at the hotel. It was quicker than I'd expected.

He couldn't have got any closer to the entrance of the hotel reception. The way he parked his car, walking was not required.

'Here already,' I said.

'Afraid so,' he replied. 'I'm 'aving a party in August. Why don't you come?' he asked in a casual half-joking way just before I got out of the car. He looked over at me. His big, cheeky grin appeared.

'Okay then,' I said, playing along.

'Good. That's settled then,' he said, tapping the steering wheel with both his hands whilst giving a nod and a smile. We both got out. Before I could take hold of my case, he darted to my side. 'Please, let me. I insist,' he said, stepping in to take it from me.

He scored highly for having manners. Consciously aware of rating him, in my mind he ticked another box. Together, we walked into the hotel.

Through the revolving doors, the large fountain situated in reception greeted us with a scent of newly mown grass. Tufts of green in the water made me think it was more likely to be the smell of fresh blooms of algae. It never reached a stale turning point of rotten cabbage. It was a proper five-star affair; the kind of place I'd previously imagined aircrew stopped at all the time. The airline must have struck a good deal. Most of the time, the reality wasn't that impressive.

We were never slumming it. But it wasn't usually plush, just comfortable and *nice*, which was *okay* or even *good*. So, this hotel was better than the usual. If I was being picky, its only downside was its breakfast being continental rather than a slap-up Glasgow feast.

I checked in. Marc waited.

'Are you coming down for a drink?' he asked.

'Why not?' I shrugged, pleased that he'd asked.

'That's the spirit,' he laughed.

'See you in ten minutes,' I said, trying to contain my flush of excitement as I stepped into the lift.

♡

The hotel bar was usually rammed and conveniently tucked away from the restaurants and most of the public. It was an air crew hangout and possibly why it had become more lax than other parts of the hotel. And packed with French crew dressed in uniform; I loved their rebellious attitude. Wearing uniform in hotel bars was forbidden by our company. In training, they'd told us how it didn't portray the correct image. I disagreed. But in true obedient Brit style, I always wore my own civvy clothes and felt fortunate that I'd recently washed and repacked something decent – cream trousers, black boots and a black off the shoulder top, which seemed fitting for a Friday night in a Parisian bar. Sexy but not too obvious.

As I entered the bar, Marc and the rest of my gang waved to me from across the room, all with pints in hand. They'd removed their identifying bits and bobs, but it was easier for them, being an all-male crew, wearing plain trousers and a white shirt. Approaching the bar, Jim cupped his hands around his mouth shouting, 'What you drinking?'

'Half a lager, thanks,' I replied.

Looking over Jim's shoulder, I glanced further down the bar.

'Pint,' Jim shouted across to Marc just as he caught my eye.

A pint of lager was passed down to me via the hands of each of the crew members. I perched on the end bar stool. Raising my glass to Marc, I thanked him, wondering whether we'd get a chance to talk, although the music volume would make it challenging.

Brown sacks of monkey nuts were dotted around the room. Piles of broken nuts littered the floor and grew bigger as I chatted to Jim. It was *shouty* chatter, the type I reverted to at nightclubs – bellowing into an eardrum, a pitch below my usual tone to try and make my words heard. I watched people cracking open nuts and throwing empty shells on the floor. Not that anyone seemed to care. With the bouncers on hand, the Parisian management were relaxed, no doubt having turned a blind eye, being used to the business and abuse from aircrew. Had it been a five-star UK hotel, someone would have complained.

'Just lob it on the floor, man,' yelled Jim.

Eager for me to join in, Jim demonstrated his proficiency with a flick of the wrist action, sending his leftover nutshell to the ground. Unaccustomed, I used the ashtray. Jim was a hooligan.

The tables started to empty, and we moved to a free spot, further away from the speakers booming out dance music. Sinking into a comfortable chair, I found Marc beside me. Jim bought the next round of drinks. The alcohol loosened my behaviour, enough to join the camaraderie of chucking my empty monkey nutshells on the floor, which was surprisingly fun.

'You should go to Marc's party,' said Henri.

His comment, directed at me, seemed to come from nowhere. Feeling the buzz of alcohol, I'd drank almost one and a half full pints of lager and I needed the loo, but it wasn't urgent. It felt a *skin-full* after a long flying day.

As a self-confessed lightweight since student days, it was apparent amongst the drinking standards of some aircrew.

I glanced at Marc and giggled.

'Well, Marc,' I said confidently, 'if I'm going to your party, I need your address.'

Marc took out the bar receipt from his pocket and wasted no time in scribbling down his details on the reverse. He passed it to me. On it he'd written his address, mobile and home telephone numbers and his email.

Positioned at an angle, my eyes craftily studied his face in detail without having to directly turn my head. I took in the appearance of his kissable full lips and wondered how they'd feel pressed against mine. I thought back to the sauce incident.

He wasn't my usual rugby type – the thicker-set, bigger-built muscle man. That wasn't Marc. But the exception was a bum that looked good in a pair of tight-fitting jeans in a *Darcy-esque* manner, and Marc had already passed the trouser test. He had a great rear view. I'd established that fact earlier, and much more... in my imagination.

Marc's hefty pilot watch flashed as he picked up his pint. Watch bling – an expensive bit of shiny couture on a man was something I liked. It suggested an interest in dress sense. But it stopped there. Other chunky jewellery, like a gold medallion soap-on-a-rope or the fat ring of a rap singer, was not my thing.

Marc's hair flopped in front of his face, curtains style. He had a look of stubble coming through this late in the day, his past five o'clock shadow, which suited him in a rugged kind of manly way. He looked about mid-thirties, much older than any man I had ever dated. But he was probably past the stage of relationship avoidance or commitment phobia that men in their twenties often suffered. Maybe in France it was different, and phobia type issues had yet to spread and infect the continent. *Did French women find him a hottie?*

The longer I looked, the more attractive he became and the more points he scored. *Was alcohol pushing up his ratings?* He wasn't typically handsome, but it didn't matter. His charismatic appeal made him strangely seductive. He exuded confidence, in the manner of a man stepping up to take charge, which I concocted in my head, probably because of his job.

'Why do you keep looking at me weird like that?' said Marc.

Oh fuck, had I been staring? Emma had warned me numerous times about my *one-eyed-snake look* – a bad, creepy habit of peeping out the corner of my eye.

'Like what?' I replied, pretending it was no big deal.

He gave me a quick demo. *Shit,* I was gutted. And Emma was right. Damn drinking so much bloody lager. *Why did I have such a freaky habit? Did he now want to retract those details he'd just given me because I was acting like some sort of freak?*

'Sorry, I was looking at the bar. I thought I recognised someone,' I said, attempting a shot at recovery, but surprising myself with on-the-spot thinking, however weak.

'And do you?' Marc said.

'What?' I said.

'Do you recognise them?' he asked.

'Urghh, nope. I thought I did but it's a bit dark in here, isn't it?' I replied, feeling stupid.

Bloody hell; I wasn't expecting a quiz. But it was apparent everyone had been *earwigging*, because they all looked in the direction of the bar.

Whilst I'd been imagining Marc naked, he'd been watching me watching him – the whole time. The naked thought lingered and made me blush. I couldn't look at him.

Marc had been elevated to the new Mr Potential, aided by beer goggles. *How did men do that?* It worked when there was absolutely no attraction to begin with. Then by some clever trickery, they made you like them. It's what I termed a *grower,* and that was Marc. There'd been no instant interest, not in the sense that I'd looked and immediately fancied the pants off him.

It never worked the other way around. Men could be *growers* but girls / women were only ever in the *yes* or *no* list from the start. That was my experience. The exception was the bedroom category. This category was only ever about a *fast fuck,* and if he thought you were willing then you were in. It was almost open to all, but you'd never become a *keeper*. He didn't even need to like you. Men made assessments based on looks. Women did the same, but opinion could shift, based on getting to know someone – personality over looks, whereas men often rated looks over personality. Girls had beauty products and hair straighteners for appearance. Personality kicked in much later to make her a *keeper*.

A left-field question from Henri disturbed my contemplative thoughts.

'What do you think I should send?' he asked me.

'What are you talking about?' I asked.

'Daniel,' Henri replied. I still wasn't following. 'You know, a text saying something nice to Daniel.'

'Come on, April. Henri wants to get his leg over with Daniel and wants your help to make it happen,' added Jim.

'Sorry, Henri,' I said, realising Jim's lack of tact and Henri's plea for help. 'I'm a bit knackered but let me have a think.'

'Yes, I understand. Working for a company like Jet Xpress you are naaykid today, naaykid tomorrow, always naaykid,' said Henri.

Who was I to correct his English when my French was terrible? I smiled, used to the little nuances from some French crew.

'Knackered… not naked!' Marc said, stepping in immediately to put him right. Suddenly it was hilarious.

'Oops. You knew what I meant,' said Henri, laughing.

Henri got out his mobile.

' 'Ow about: the weather is beautiful, wish you were 'ere with me? Don't you think that's romantic?' Marc said. His eyes directed that question at me, with a smile. 'Wouldn't you like to get a text saying that? They're words from my favourite song.'

'Sounds like a postcard message,' I replied, trying not to look too impressed. *What was his favourite song?* Clearly, he was a charmer, but I hoped he wasn't a *player*.

'You could be anywhere,' Marc said, and shrugged his shoulders.

'That's brilliant, man,' said Jim. 'Think *I* might send that to *my* girlfriend. That should score me some points.'

Henri, all enthused with Marc's suggestion, eagerly began tapping out his message.

'You don't think it's too much?' Henri turned to me. 'Do you think he's gonna like that?'

'That's probably gonna do the trick for you, Henri,' I replied.

Marc caught my eye again. We smiled.

'You've got to tell us if this comes off. Marc, I think I'm gonna name you King of Gay Text,' Jim announced as he slapped Henri on the back.

'Not sure that's much of a compliment to an 'eterosexual male,' Marc said.

We all laughed.

'I thought you were sending it to your girlfriend,' I reminded Jim.

'It's versatile,' Jim replied.

'Sent,' said Henri, proudly holding up his mobile.

Henri and Jim started to chat again. Then Marc leaned in close towards me.

'Tell me about yourself,' he said.

The low sound of his foreign voice made me nervous. I couldn't think what to say. I reached for my hair and coiled a section around my finger. His big brown eyes drifted down to rest on my body. I clasped my hands together. My palms felt sweaty. The drink was no longer having a lasting effect. I could feel him, watching me. He made me feel exposed and vulnerable, the way he looked at me. I folded my arms across my chest.

'There's not really much to tell,' I said.

The high-pitched squeakiness of my voice surprised me, and I hated it. I drew a breath and tried to *get a grip*, struggling to keep cool. But as Marc sat back in his chair, I immediately began to relax.

'What are your ambitions then?' Marc said, his body tilting forward towards mine.

I drew another breath.

'Well, I'd like to learn to fly. I wouldn't mind learning to play the piano, but as I can't fit a piano into my flat I'll settle for the guitar. I'd also like to write a novel, learn French and run the London marathon,' I blurted out.

I surprised even myself with the marathon running. It had never been a goal I was consciously aware of, until now. But still, I was pleased at having rolled off a list of ambitions in an articulate fashion. Then I congratulated myself on having not sprayed him with speckles of spit when I'd talked.

The effects of drinking more than one pint were often that I lost control of my ability to talk without accidentally spitting and shouting. Not outrageously. But according to Emma, I got noticeably louder than was necessary.

'I can play the piano,' he said.

'Really. Maybe you can teach me then?' I said, concentrating hard to avoid both shouting and spitting at him.

'Sure. Only by ear. I'm not good at it.' He smiled at me. 'But I could teach you French. Then I'll teach you how to fly and after that we'll go learn to play the guitar together!' He laughed.

Clearly, he'd graduated from charm school with a diploma and possibly written a manual or two. But hooked on his attention, I wanted more.

'And what about running?' I reminded him.

'That's easy. I ran the Paris marathon last year, so we can go running together,' he said.

A smoker and a runner, how did that work? I was convinced that with all my yoga I was bound to be fitter than him.

'You 'ave an unusual name, April,' he said.

'Yes. Nothing to do with me. All down to my folks. They wanted something to do with being a springtime baby, and it fits my surname. It's the Latin for *to open* meaning *buds*, like my surname,' I said.

'Really. I like it. So, the French version is *Avril*. You like that?' he asked.

'I like how you say it,' I replied. *Why was I so obviously slobbering with lust?*

It wasn't a good time for a toilet exit, ruining the ambience to nip off for a quick wee. But I'd been cross-legged for a while, and aware of the increasing urge, I couldn't wait. There was never going to be a convenient time. Once I started on lager, it was approximately twenty-minute stints to the loo. I'd discovered a certain technique for prolonging the timed gaps – holding off for as long as possible the first time around, then increasing them to thirty-minutes, which avoided the frequency of visits, so long as no one told a funny joke.

Emma and I first tested this theory in the pub one night. We played a stupid game after making a ridiculous bet over who could hold out the longest. Laughing usually made her wee with the force of a horse. (Privacy was almost impossible in a hollow-walled flat.) But after bursting into the cubicles together, she held out to win until finally pissing Niagara Falls.

'Excuse me,' I said.

'Of course,' Marc replied, moving his chair aside to clear an exit.

Walking in a straight line required a steady focus. Trying hard not to look fuddled, it wasn't easy to attempt my most eloquent strut whilst simultaneously squeezing everything hard to prevent a dam from busting open.

On my return, I bought the final drinks round. Feeling hammered, I ordered a large water. The crew numbers had thinned. Throwing-out time was approaching, and no one was going to argue with the beefy black bouncer on patrol, encouraging everyone to finish their drinks, which we all did.

In the lobby, Marc met with more airline staff. A small crowd of three pretty French *hosties* flocked to Marc like a magnet. His easy-going nature around women was evident. He chatted confidently, even though I couldn't understand a word. They didn't notice me. There was too much giggling.

'Bye, Marc,' I said with a raised voice, as I turned to leave with the others.

'Wait. One moment, Avril,' said Marc. 'I 'ave to get the lift too. My car is parked basement level.'

He raised his hand to say goodbye to the group and strolled towards me. I felt smug. We walked towards the lift together. As the doors opened, he gently placed his hand on the curve of my lower spine, as if to guide me through. A tingle rushed through my body. Then he removed his hand as naturally as he'd placed it. All four of us got in.

The June heat was intensified in the close confines of the lift space shared between four bodies. It made my head woozy. As the lift moved down to the basement level car park, I experienced a similar sensation in my stomach to being on a fairground ride. It churned with too much booze.

'What a night,' Jim began. 'Marc's sorted it out for Henri to get his end away, and he's not done badly with you.'

Jim poked his finger into my shoulder. I tapped him back. Then I shot an awkward glance at Marc, feeling embarrassed by Jim's remark. Marc looked at Jim with a grin.

'Do you promise you're coming to my party? I might be disappointed if you didn't,' Marc said, his face beaming at me.

'Seal the deal,' Jim said.

I needed no encouragement. The forced proximity of our bodies seemed to enable me to shed regard for usual inhibitions.

'I think I'm just going to give you a French kiss,' I announced audibly, louder than I'd anticipated.

Marc's eyes almost sprang out of his head. It didn't deter me. Tiptoeing up to him, I pressed my lips together and planted a fat kiss on each cheek. Instantly, this was met with a *woooooo* sound from the other two, and a loud clap. Then Jim went one step further and raised his index finger in an upright direction, attempting to show... well, it was obvious.

'There's your promise,' I said.

The lift arrived and before Marc stepped out he said, 'Wait. I don't 'ave *your* number.'

'I might email you,' I replied.

Pushing the button for the second-floor bedrooms, as the doors began to close, I waved goodbye, knowing I had every intention of following up. Stepping out of the lift, Jim and I had a customary hug before strolling to our rooms.

Flinging myself onto my bed, I scoffed the half-eaten chocolate I'd left there earlier. Alcohol always gave me the munchies, and the monkey nuts hadn't plugged a gap. Lying back on the bed and studying the bar receipt containing Marc's details in my hand, I grinned and felt awesome.

The kiss had been classy, considering. There hadn't been time to worry about accidentally dribbling or fumigating beer breath. Perhaps I'd have ravaged him if we'd been alone with a full-on tongues Frenchie washing-machine style, although I doubted I'd have had the nerve.

I grappled in my bag for my mobile and composed a text:

Amazin nite Ems. Just kissed a frog. Giv u the goss l8r obvs.

I'd dissect the finer details with Emma at home.

Pizza, Parties and Plans

I put the key in the lock and the door swung open, almost taking me with it.

'Oh my God, oh my God. So, what happened?' Emma said, simultaneously stuffing her face with pizza and forcing words out of her mouth.

'I'll tell you *all* about it,' I said.

I straightened myself up, after having nearly fallen into the porch. The speed of the door being swung open so unexpectedly fast had almost caused me to topple over. She'd obviously heard my car pull up onto our drive.

'Wine first and I'm starvin'. Any of that pizza left?' I asked.

She handed me the remainder of hers. But seeing the bite marks and imprint of teeth left in the cheese made me change my mind.

'What's he like?' she asked. 'You didn't even tell me you liked anyone. Is he a good snog? Come on, I'm dying to know. I've had to wait all this time for you to get home.'

Dumping my case in the hallway and kicking off my shoes, I ran upstairs then jumped onto the sofa, landing on the stack of fluffy cushions. She followed me, almost landing on top.

Our flat was on the first floor, which we'd renamed the Penthouse. It was small but adequate for us. Emma had already laid out our Saturday night supplies on the table by the TV, next to the 007 gun for our favourite game of smoking hot cocktails, James Bond style. There were two glasses, wine in the cooler – fizzy – pizza (what was left of it) and crisps. Our all-time favourite ice cream – *pralines and cream* – was in the freezer, I'd bought it on my last shopping trip. We had everything we needed to accompany a most important, lengthy and in-depth discussion followed by a quiz on tonight's new hot topic, Marc.

'Was it a tongue-twister or more of the subtle variety?' she asked, pretending to snog the back of her hand.

'It was eloquent actually,' I said in a pretend posh accent. 'You'd have been proud of me, even if I was a bit drunk. I kissed him on each cheek.' I demonstrated on Emma. She immediately wiped her face, which also removed a trace of tomato and a few crumbs of pizza.

'He gives me that tingly feeling, you know,' I said, patting my heart as I spoke.

'*Ooh la la*... yeah, that's called common sense leaving your body,' she said.

I raised two fingers.

'Then did you make mad passionate lurvvve?' she said in a husky voice and pushed me horizontal on the sofa, climbing on top.

'Weirdo,' I said, rolling her off onto the floor as she yelled and started laughing.

'I didn't shag him,' I said, 'although he does have enormous *shaggability* potential. It was *just a kiss*. Well, two actually. Only on each cheek.'

'Steady on there,' she said.

'Don't judge me by your own standards, or lack of,' I replied, as we laughed.

Whilst we ate and drank, I filled her in on everything. I told her about him progressing through the ranks from huge teeth to mighty sex god – although it hadn't yet been tested out. I related minute details of how he brushed his floppy dark hair out of his face with a hand-stroke and cute flick of his head and that he'd renamed me the French version of my name, *Avril*. And that he was having a party.

'Avril?' Emma repeated, questioning the name by screwing her face up.

'A party?' Emma asked, 'like a proper French style party in gay Paree?' She gesticulated with her hands, pretending to smoke a very long cigarette.

'Yes, except I don't know anything about it so far, other than I've got his details and it's sometime in August,' I said.

'He sounds suave. Come, my cherie. We 'ave work to do to get you a little French amour,' Emma said, leading me to the computer where she plonked me down at the chair.

She shoved a glass into my hand and grabbed the bottle of fizz. Clumsily, she poured so fast that it rose to the top of the rim, bubbled up then spilled over the edge onto my hand, then the floor.

'Careful,' I said, grabbing the bottle from her. 'If we've only got one bottle, we can't afford to waste it.'

'Arghh, oo carez. Anyway, we still ave ze gun for ze cocktails,' she said in a dodgy accent, raising her shoulders, strangely enough in the same way Marc had done when discussing working in the chicken factory.

'What are you doing? Why have you sat me here?' I asked.

'Homework,' Emma said in a more serious tone. 'Clearly, you have it bad for this guy. We need to plan what you're going to send. You have his email, right?'

'Yes, but…'

'And you want to see him again and maybe go to a little soiree in Paris and do a bit more than kissing on the cheek next time?' she continued.

I laughed. 'Possibly… okay, yeah.'

'Well, you're going to have to send him the first message soon as you didn't give him anything. So, get logging on. We need to make sure you get it right. That's where I come in, Doctor Lurve,' she said. When Emma had a plan, it was usually crazy. But I went along with it. 'Come on, drink a bit more of that sparkly and let's get creative and dream up something hot to send.'

I gulped the wine. 'I can't send him a message yet; I've only just finished working with him.'

'Aha. Yes, but you can have it planned out right now and we'll keep it in your drafts ready. This is so much fun,' she said and clapped her hands. I rolled my eyes. 'Oh, *come on*. You *know* you need a bit of help with this. You're more fun on beer, works faster, pity we've ran out.'

'Actually, I'm not doing too badly by myself so far,' I said.

But she was right. I usually knew how to mess things up. Like the time I went on a date, got a bit too drunk and ended up vomiting on a guy's shoes as he stood on the pavement watching. Thankfully, I never saw him again.

'Right, move over. The love doctor needs to get to work,' she said.

She shoved me off the seat, spilling more wine, and dominated the computer. There was no way I'd share his contact information with her. Who knew what she might do in her attempts to fix me up? But I'd let her tap out a message. She was usually the witty one. Anyway, I could always alter it later. After a couple of hours (it took us that long to craft a few simple sentences), and me having scrapped most of Emma's wild attempts at a hot message, she resigned herself to bed for the night. I sat and pored over our combined but carefully composed attempt.

From: *April@redhotmail.co.uk*
To:
Subject: *Bonjour!*

Salut Marc!

    Thought I'd test out those details you gave me!

    It was good to have your company on the Paris night-stop. I hadn't been looking forward to it, but it was a good crew and a fun night in the bar.

    I've got a couple of standby days on my roster coming up, so I may find myself in Paris again before the end of the month… be great to see you again.

    Don't work too hard.

    April x

I added a kiss, hopefully reminding him of the lift episode, although it was unlikely he'd forget. The plan or golden rule was to let four days lapse, because that amount of time avoided a look of *desperado*.

What a relief email existed! It was preferable to a potentially difficult and stilted phone conversation. There was no way I'd do that… too many pitfalls. This way it could be *tailored to perfection*, as Emma had said. Light and casual yet considered and meticulously prepared.

That level of effort never went into application forms, but usually no one filled them out for me either. I'd recently applied for a long-haul position just to try my luck, and it hadn't taken me nearly as long to complete.

I reread the email to Marc, just to make sure the words hadn't somehow jumbled themselves up a bit, like predictive text. I was still traumatised from having received an awkward message from my mum one night, about my parents having *fondled* themselves, meaning *Googled* their names.

Two days passed; it was Monday morning and my final rest day. Sitting alone in pyjamas, I contemplated sending the message to Marc. I'd thought about him. Unable to resist, I booted up the computer, filled in the *to* line. Then on impulse hit *send*.

A pang of excitement raced through me as it disappeared off my screen. My message had left England and was flying over the Channel to Paris, France. The concocted four-day rule had been wiped out by impatience. Biting my fingernail, I wondered when he'd get it. *Did he check his mail regularly? Or was he the annoying type that left it for ages?* I texted Emma: *The deed's done.* Secretly, she'd be pleased, despite breaking the agreed golden formula, which had no proven past results, and she was just as impatient.

After two days and no reply, my logical reasoning vanished. I began overanalysing that maybe he wasn't really interested. Perhaps he'd had a bet on with Henri that night. Maybe he was one of *those* pilots.

Only a minority of pilots had an ego with a head size to match. And some *hosties* were willing to be a bike to bag one. Kerrie, the gorgeous goddess from my first day, had become a well-known social butterfly. After having got her well-manicured claws into Christian for starters, she'd soon moved on to pilots as a main course, or so the rumours went. Christian was also a distant memory for me.

There were other obvious gold-digger *hosties*. But ironically, the young and attractive pilots were usually in heaps of debt. The silver foxes (grey, wizened and so old they were off my scale) could afford to be more generous at the bar.

My over-thinking led to a dangerous tango with the keyboard. Hurriedly, I bashed out a prompt.

From:	*April@redhotmail.co.uk*
To:	*Marc@worldawayonline.fr*
Subject:	*Bonjour again!*

I forgot to mention your party. If it's a definite I'd love to come! If you'd like to get in touch it would be great to hear from you.

Mobile: 00153 6079786099
April x

I hit *send*. Instantly, I regretted it, for being such a loser. Emma would call me a *muppet*. I cringed and decided to try and forget all about it.

♡

After a couple more days, two replies arrived.

From:	*Marc@worldawayonline.fr*
To:	*April@redhotmail.co.uk*
Subject:	*Re: Bonjour!*

Hello Avril

Good to hear from you. You did the right thing by getting in touch. I just got back from doing the earlies. I'm away on night-stops until Monday. Hopefully they'll send you to Paris CDG on your standbys. Let me know if you get called out, that will be nice to meet again. Next time we'll try to find a good restaurant. Got to get some sleep so will say goodnight now.

Hopefully talk to you very soon.

Marc x

The next one read:

From:	*Marc@worldawayonline.fr*
To:	*April@redhotmail.co.uk*
Subject:	*Re: Bonjour again!*

Just got your new email.

Of course you're welcome for the party, it's Sunday
August 24th my place, please come.

Night again xx

Two kisses. I smiled. That night, I recounted everything
to Emma.

'Don't worry. Guys don't analyse in the same way
that girls go over every last thing there is to examine,'
Emma said. 'He's probably too knackered to notice how
uncool you are. It's not like he's tucked up in bed with
a mug of hot chocolate by 10 pm each night thinking
about you.'

'Harsh but true,' I replied. Emma always spoke bluntly,
even if her words smacked and bruised occasionally.

'Anyway. I can't wait. I'm going to a proper ooh la la
French party,' she said.

'You mean *I'm* going to a French party,' I said, puzzled.

'But you know you're going to need me to hold
your hand. If he's having a party then he's not going to
be able to spend all his time with you, and you'll hardly
know anyone. And you can't even speak French. He'll be
busy entertaining and juggling baguettes and garlic and
whatever French people do at parties,' Emma said, whilst
giving me a demo of pretend juggling with the DVDs on
her lap, which ended up on the floor.

We looked through our mixed collection of DVDs
/ VHS cassettes, trying to decide on a film. I favoured
Indecent Proposal. Emma wanted *Ghost*. We'd seen them
both a *zillion* times, but it didn't stop us watching them
on repeat. We'd seen *Desperately Seeking Susan* on video

cassette exactly fifteen times as teenagers, just because we thought it made us true Madonna fans.

We kept a relegation shelf containing all the films we couldn't agree on (mainly science fiction, which was Emma's stuff, and an occasional documentary, which was mine). That shelf was strictly for nights in by yourself. It was past 10 pm, and giving in to *Ghost*, I knew I'd be asleep before the end.

'You can just tell him I'll be coming with you,' she continued. 'The rate you're churning out these messages, you'll be virtually engaged to him by then anyway.'

'Need to test drive him first and go on a date,' I laughed.

'And that's your next email. We'll do it tomorrow,' Emma said, 'after skating.'

'I'll do it myself.'

'Oh, let me. I'm so enjoying this and just when it's starting to get good,' she said. 'A French love machine and an English rose. Don't worry, I'm not imagining you two or anything… not that I know what he looks like. But I've got a sort of sugar daddy, Gerard Depardieu, image going on.'

'Eww. He's not that old, or ugly, and I might just want to keep a few things private. Sorry, but you know…'

I hugged the DVD close to my chest.

'You're spoiling my fun,' she said with a grin.

I developed a bad crush and went off food. I couldn't physically force myself to eat. It wasn't a problem at work;

the cardboard crew meals weren't that appetising anyway. But I just wasn't hungry. I was content living on lust and allowing my heart to rule my head, like a teenager. Marc was on my mind.

The sleep deprivation made it worse. I'd worked more charter flights as the summer season began. Sometimes I was too wired, like an over-exhausted toddler – knackered but unable to drop off. The rumoured effect was premature ageing, which worried me, if the looks of the dragon wagons were anything to judge by. Shift work gave us a certain tired-all-the-time look. Plastering on a layer of make-up became an art form of disguise, mainly hiding bags under eyes. But I'd worry about my face dropping and bits and pieces sagging, further down the line. For now, a Wonderbra, moisturiser and a good concealer hid any damage.

For most of the day, I'd been seeking inspiration for something to write to Marc. Perhaps I could tell him about the new charter flight to Corsica. When we flew over Bastia, I'd gazed out of the window and caught a glimpse of the tiny aquamarine coloured pools as they sparkled amongst a backdrop of mountainous rock formations. The sunlight glimmered off the surface; it was stunning. The sky had been a perfect sapphire holiday blue. Marc would understand. He'd appreciate the beauty in flying. From the cockpit, he'd have a *birdseye* view.

I'd promised myself two things on that flight. Firstly, I would look up where Corsica was on a map. (My geography was terrible, but I would rectify that later.) Secondly, one day I would holiday there.

The Bastia trip outweighed the Ibiza charters. It was easier. The clientele was more upmarket, attracting discerning older couples and families rather than a budget flight to Ibiza. Those flights were frequented by a three-star fake tan and alcohol crowd looking to drink the bars dry. And the alcohol mixed with altitude worked more potently up in the sky, resulting in lively passengers and hard work.

It was past 11 pm. I clicked on a new message, leaving the subject line blank. I didn't bother telling Marc about Corsica in an email. It felt stupid.

From: *April@redhotmail.co.uk*
To: *Marc@worldawayonline.fr*
Subject:

Hi Marc

It was great to hear from you. I hope you got some sleep on those night-stops? I did a late charter to Italy and didn't get back till 5.30 am last week. As Henri would say – I was "naaykid"!

Let me know if you have a free day, maybe we could meet up? It would be great to see you.

Au Revoir

April xx

Being brave by email wasn't a problem. Awkward moments didn't exist. I thought about the old lady on the plane, then added a P.S.

P.S When are you going to give me that French lesson!

From: *Marc@worldawayonline.fr*
To: *April@redhotmail.co.uk*
Subject: *Re:*

Hello Avril

Night-stops in Guernsey not too bad, thanks for asking but good to get back. Pretty busy July roster but we should definitely find time to meet.

I'll teach you French anytime, you just need to come over to France, it's easier to learn in the country… not joking, plus more sunshine on this side of the Channel.

Got to go, speak soon

Marc xx

I got up uncharacteristically early after a late finish. But I couldn't sleep in. The sun beamed through the kitchen window as I stood in the rays, waiting for the kettle to boil. Closing my eyes and feeling the warmth bathe my skin, I smiled. Visiting him in Paris was an idea I loved, along with him becoming my French teacher.

My mind drifted as I thought about his email and sipped my tea. I knew the tired old hotel in Guernsey where he'd stayed. It was unlike most other places. It was vintage and similar to a rustic French hotel. Breakfast was served in its huge dining room with its distinctive green forest-coloured velvet curtains, finished off with swags and pelmets – (something I'd learned about from my gran talking about her interiors, along with carpets and curtains which I'd since relegated to the world of domestic boredom). There were old woven rugs on the floor and curvaceous ancient wooden chairs. Heavy linen magnolia tablecloths were laid out with matching napkins, which stood in a fan shape at each place setting. The shiny cutlery was ornate, and there were tiny bowls of brown and white sugar cubes, with a little silver sugar server in the middle of the table – the type found in an antique shop. I imagined older clientele feeling at home. I wondered if Marc liked it.

The door creaked open.

'So, what's the latest in your romantic saga?' said Emma, interrupting my thoughts.

She filled her bowl with cornflakes, glimpsing at the TV she'd just turned on, whilst sheltering her eyes from the sunlight and trying to talk to me all at the same time. Sensory overload was typical of Emma.

'I suggested meeting up. I'm thinking of phoning him. What do you reckon?' I asked.

'Ooh. Things *have* progressed. But ooh… a phone call? You sure about that? Could be tricky,' she said. Emma became busy shovelling mountains of cornflakes into her mouth, which didn't prevent her from speaking. She paused briefly, then said, 'You know what… do it. What you gonna say?' She looked at me for a response, taking a break from her noisy crunching.

'Why the sudden change?' I asked.

'Well, you may as well go for it. He likes you… you like him…'

She rocked a spoon in her hand, backwards and forwards, as she spoke.

'Well, I'm gonna get it all planned out, just in case the conversation dries up. Optimum planning and maximum effort to ensure no awkwardness,' I said and took another sip of tea contemplating what to say.

'So funny. That's you all right. Taking care of every detail. I should try that some time. Anyway, gotta rush. Love ya,' she said and disappeared off, taking her bowl of cereal as she went. 'Good luck,' she shouted from her bedroom.

'I'm not doing it until Saturday,' I called, 'more chance of catching him.'

I got out a notebook from the kitchen drawer and started to scribble some prompts. I put stuff on there like work, weekend plans and drew a ring around spare time – a need to know, so we could meet. Other than flying, I wondered if he had many interests. *Did he have other women in his life?* I hoped not. I thought about the women in the Paris bar and jabbed my pencil into the paper. Trying to dismiss jealous thoughts, I reminded myself to pick out the CD, *Chilled-Out 80s*. Background music was necessary as a relaxed distraction, better for the flow of conversation.

It was Saturday at 6.50 pm. I planned to ring after 7 pm UK time, making it 8 pm in Paris. It was all detailed on the notepad with military precision. I'd calculated that if he were planning to go out, I'd catch him beforehand. I had no firm affirmations of his plans. My only rationale or logic was that it was a Saturday night in Paris. And if he wasn't working then I guessed that he'd probably be going somewhere, whilst I, on the other hand, had absolutely no plans and wasn't going anywhere.

Running over a potential conversation in my head, I had my list of prompts to hand. Nervously excited, I scrolled through my mobile as far as the name *Marc* then pressed *call*. I listened to the sound of the international ringtone, my ear firmly pressed to my mobile as jitters filled my stomach. With its long tones, it confirmed that

I was ringing abroad. It rang three times, making me start to wonder if it would divert to voicemail.

'Allo.'

I felt a surge of adrenaline.

'Oh hi. Is that Marc?' I asked shyly, more nervous than I thought. 'It's April.'

Like a cold caller, I waited for his response. Holding the mobile to my ear felt like listening to my own heartbeat.

'Avril. Hi… just a moment… I 'ave someone on the other line… just a moment. I'll put that one down and be straight back with you.'

Prioritising me over someone else was a good sign. I smiled. There were faint mumblings of French in the background.

'Sorry about that. Just 'ad another call. So, 'ow are you?' he asked.

'Fine, thanks. And how are you?' I replied, smiling.

'I'm off work at the moment. Got a problem with my eardrum, means I can't fly.'

'Oh, I'm sorry to hear that,' I said.

'It's okay.'

There was a pause whilst I wondered whether to question him further about eardrums or to just ignore it.

'How long have you been off work?' I asked.

'About only three days so far, but I'm not going back until my ears get better. So, what 'ave you been doing with yourself?' he asked.

The pitch of his voice was raised. I could sense that he was smiling at the other end.

'Well, I survived skating with my flatmate Emma.'

'Skating?' he asked.

'Yes, skating. I have a flatmate called Emma. She's big on going to yoga, usually. We both are. But I went skating with her the other night. She thought it would be fun to try something different. It was a roller-disco. No kids allowed, except us. So we had a good go.'

He laughed.

'And you still 'ave your legs intact?' he asked.

'Actually, I'm not too bad,' I insisted. 'I lived at the skating rink as a teenager.'

'Maybe you can show me some time,' he said.

'Definitely. I wouldn't mind watching you on a pair of skates.'

'It would be bad news, I think,' he said.

There was another pause. I consulted my list of prompts.

'Well, I was just ringing to find out if you were free sometime soon, but I didn't realise you were ill.'

'Listen. I can't fly, but I'm okay. I was gonna email you tonight.'

'I think you still should,' I said.

'I was gonna suggest dates for meeting up. 'Ow about Paris?' he asked.

'Well, if you're sure you're okay. Maybe we could meet for a day.'

'Sure… but just one day? You'll spend most of it travelling. If you want to plan on spending a few days, you can stay 'ere, and I'll show you round France. It's up to you,' he said.

'Okay,' I replied, feeling uncertain. I hadn't expected him to suggest a few days. I'd thought a casual meet-up and lunch perhaps, for a first date. 'How about sometime next weekend?' The words rolled out of my mouth before my brain had fully engaged. 'I'm working Saturday but off Sunday, Monday.'

'Whenever you want. Just let me know what flight you're on and I'll come and pick you up at the airport,' he said.

'Okay. I'll let you know,' I said.

'Okay. I look forward to seeing you. Speak soon.'

'Don't forget to send that email anyway,' I reminded him.

I listened for him to hang up. But instead in the background I heard him say *merde*. And even I recognised that terminology in French.

'Is everything okay?' I asked.

'Oh, it's all right. I just burnt the sauce for my steak.'

'So, you're not a good cook then?' I joked.

'I do okay. I'll show you when you come over,' he laughed.

'Okay. Speak to you soon – bye.'

I hung up. And just like that, an international hot date in Paris was set.

Then doubt crept in. *What if things turned awkward? What if we didn't get on? What if it turned to disaster and I was stuck out there?*

THE RENDEZVOUS

July 2003

As I flew down the motorway in my *Mini,* my sunglasses averted the bright sunshine filtering through. I twisted the volume knob to maximum and belted out the lyrics to Bon Jovi's *Living on a Prayer.* And my CD pounded off the interior metal of the car, making it tin-pot deafening. I loved it.

Driving to the airport listening to music with no restrictions on noise, unlike in the Penthouse, meant I took full advantage. On the motorway, my *Mini* was like an electric racing go cart. Each dent of the road surface made it bounce along. The height of the traffic surrounding me, especially lorries, made the whole car feel totally unsuitable for long journeys. But I was used to it. And even though I was heavy footed on the right pedal, it took its time to build speed. But with a bit of concentration, I could get the needle to sit around eighty.

The traffic was light, which was usual for a Sunday. But despite there being no rush, it seemed to take forever to reach the airport, no matter how hard I stepped on the accelerator. The air conditioning was switched to cold, although it was never cool, just not as hot as pushing the control in the other direction.

The excitement of going to Paris gave me the jitters. My stomach flipped a fast somersault every time I thought about Marc. Approaching the airport, I wound down my window and took one eye off the road. A plane was taking off into a perfect blue setting. It climbed like they do with its nose to the sky. When it soared high enough, the magical vapour trail poured out behind like the foam of sparkling bubbles seeping down an overfull glass of fresh champagne. High on nervous energy, I giggled. *What hot-blooded woman can resist the allure of a good-looking and seductive Frenchman?* Not me, that was for sure.

The airline desk dished out my staff ticket and it all became more real by the minute – yet so surreal in equal measures. Endorphins kicked at the pit of my stomach as I realised that I'd arrive in Paris in less than two hours. Instinctively, I headed up to the crew room. It wasn't necessary. But being familiar, I thought I'd wait there before departures. Had I considered things more carefully, then perhaps being sat with other passengers was more sensible. But I was carefree. It wasn't until I saw Becky in the crew room that I realised I was unprepared. It prompted me to invent a fabricated *bullshit* story, just in case of nosiness – visiting a friend, not anyone connected with the airlines. It was my business and wiser not to tell. Not aircrew. I imagined the gossip and how easy it was to become the latest victim of idol rumours and ending up as one of Jim's stories. That wasn't happening. Marc was my special secret.

Becky didn't even notice me. She left sharpish, almost getting her fluorescent jacket trapped in the doorframe as she rushed out. I relaxed back on the sofa; there were no stories necessary now. At home it was different. Sharing stuff with Emma was not only mandatory but crucial. I needed a confidante.

The flight was on time. And on boarding, my colleagues weren't familiar, which was fortunate.

'Hi, you positioning to Paris today?' said a crew member. I knew her name was Rachel, but I didn't *know* her.

'Just visiting a friend,' I said casually. *She seemed to buy it, but why wouldn't she?* I tried to relax but couldn't. Nervous energy flew round my body at a rate of knots. I rubbed the sweat from my palms on the lap of my smart blue jeans.

Dark jeans looked good on me, making my legs seem longer than the lighter coloured pair, which I reserved for cleaning jobs around the Penthouse. Even though it was a hot day, I opted to wear jeans when flying off duty – a must-have flying companion, disguising sweat patches and crumples.

Dressed in heeled sandals and a dark low-cut top felt suggestively sex kitten, but not overdone. Freely, I spritzed on a cloud of *Coco Chanel Mademoiselle* perfume. Moderation and toilet water were not required. I wasn't working this flight.

Below the outerwear, I was hoisted up in my new underwear – a little black lacy number called *Annie*. When coupled with my red stilettos, a transformation into *Bad Annie*, sexy seductress, occurred in the mirror. But a less obvious look for a first date seemed the best option. I left them off. The *filthy fuck-me heels* were travelling in the case.

Strapped in, I wriggled, trying to get comfortable. I popped another mint chew into my mouth, hoping it would act as a distraction. My ample cleavage almost spilled over the top of the balcony bra – a tricky effect that had needed careful adjustment to hold my boobs with just the right amount of tension. The tight strap dug in. *Damned Annie.* I couldn't wait to tear her off and break free. And despite having lost the thong buried between my cheeks, I sported a neatly trimmed topiary garden, complete with a waxed landing strip.

Preparation had become a priority after Emma had thrown a pack of *dobbers* into my case. She'd quoted a line about *a happy and healthy, not herpes, sex life* (having picked it up from a poster at the *GUM clinic),* and her advice was to bang whomever I wanted, so long as he wore a jacket.

Her interest in my potential sex life was the reason I'd put myself through a bloody agonising hour of waxing delicate parts of anatomy that had screamed to be left alone. I'd never intended to go *au naturelle,* but I was reminded how I needed to look good down there too, meaning more than a trim. It had taken gritted teeth to perform. But a perfectly primped bush was the result.

The seatbelt sign illuminated. The crew made their landing announcement. I checked my appearance in my compact mirror, then reapplied my pink lipstick. Then I checked again, making sure my teeth weren't coated *vampire style.* My hair fell in waves over my shoulders, which had taken a heap of time to volume up and give the appearance of being loose. But I'd applied a ton of hairspray to get it rigidly right.

As the plane touched down on the tarmac, I performed the breath sniff test. Discreetly, I licked then sniffed the back of my hand. All was good.

But what if he doesn't turn up? What if he changes his mind about the whole thing? It was too late to go back. We'd arranged to meet in arrivals. If he didn't show, then the fall-back option was shopping in the centre of Paris.

I walked through arrivals biting my lip. As I looked up, Marc was waiting. Suddenly my legs felt stiff and awkward. I bumbled over. He smiled, with a brief fleeting glance. When our eyes met, I could sense that he was anxious too.

'You came,' he said.

Then I knew he'd experienced the exact same thought process, excluding the part about shopping in Paris. If I'd have been a no-show, I guessed he'd have seen his mates.

'You invited me, remember?' I said, smiling.

He leaned in for a continental-style kiss, on each cheek. Instinctively, I closed my eyes as he leaned across me. A tingling sensation took hold of my body as I breathed in his musky scent.

'You look nice,' he said, reaching for my bag.

I looked down at my feet, feeling a sudden paralyzing nervousness that I hadn't expected. Hiding behind my smile, the voice inside my head reminded me to try and act normal and stay calm.

'It's this way to my car. Was it a good flight?' he asked, as we strolled awkwardly towards the car park.

'Yes, thanks. It was nice, no delays,' I replied.

I grinned at Marc, not quite believing I was with him on a date in Paris.

'Did you tell anyone what you were doing?' he asked.

'Not any work colleagues. They don't need to know,' I said.

He nodded.

'You?' I asked.

'No,' he replied.

'Obviously, I told a friend, just in case you turned out to be an axe murderer or something. They've got your details, just to warn you,' I said.

'*Merde.* That's my plan out of the window then,' he laughed.

It didn't take long to reach his car. I stood by the passenger door and waited.

'You don't want to do the driving today?' he said, prompting me to think about him having driven me to the hotel that night.

'Stop teasing me. Anyway, I'm not good at driving on the wrong side,' I said.

We laughed.

'It's not far to my place. I 'ave champagne waiting for us in the fridge,' he said. My eyes must have lit up. 'You like champagne,' he said as more of a statement than question.

'Champagne would be nice, thank you,' I said, stupidly trying to act cool, although it wasn't working. It wasn't just the outside temperature making me melt.

He wasn't letting down the reputation of the French. I bet he had the proper stuff, not just sparkly or *pink fizz* like mine and Emma's alternative version of champagne. He was a smooth operator. Emma would be well impressed. *Who didn't like champagne? Hardcore beer drinkers perhaps?* Unless you counted getting tipsy on night-stops, there was nothing hardcore about my drinking.

'Are you 'ungry?' he asked.

Course I wasn't. Nerves had quashed any hunger pangs, even though I'd only eaten a nibble of stale airport sandwich and I'd digested half a packet of chewy mints.

'Are you going to try and impress me with your cooking skills or get me drunk on champagne, so I won't notice if you burn the sauce?' I asked.

'Both!' he replied.

As he drove us, I watched him out of the corner of my eye, the way I'd been told not to by Emma, but I couldn't resist. He looked so self-assured as he sat upright with a strong grip on the steering wheel and grin on his face. I bet he flew planes in much the same way, taking charge of the throttle.

He opened the glovebox and fumbled around for a bit, and I managed a large stare, without him noticing. He brought out a CD, held it up and looked across.

''Ave a listen,' he said, slotting it into the player.

His music was unfamiliar, but it had a calm feel to it, reminding me of Classic FM. By contrast, I doubted he'd think much of my eighties compilations and occasional dance tracks.

'Do you like it?' he asked.

'It's nice,' I nodded. Everything was becoming *nice*. I made a mental note to stop using that word. His presence escalated my self-consciousness and my vocabulary became limited.

Fidgeting in my seat, the second he told me the name of the artist on the CD, the instant I forgot. My bra was still uncomfortable.

'You okay?' he asked.

The damned bra was too tight, but I needed it clasped firm and tort, to support my chest in the right position. What I hadn't accounted for was the heat causing things to swell.

'All good,' I lied, ready to explode.

'My place is about twenty minutes away. Shouldn't take long, there's not much traffic around today,' he said.

He looked across at me with his big toothy characteristic grin. I forced a smile. The thought of another twenty minutes at least in tight lingerie made me feel less sexy super-babe and more like a sausage in a pan.

I hoped Marc was worth the discomfort. I rested my elbow on the window as we chatted. Focusing on the views, I tried to forget about *Annie*. But the main roads and traffic were not inspiring. Eventually, we turned into a tree-lined road.

' 'Ere it is,' he said, pulling up outside a quaint house, nothing like I'd pictured.

It wasn't a Parisian apartment, but we weren't in the centre. We were rural, and a good distance from central Paris. It was a countryside home, with a courtyard full of plants and flowers, making me wonder if he'd borrowed a place to impress me. He didn't seem the green-fingered type or an avid gardener. But I liked it much better than any city apartment.

'This is 'ome, for now at least… it's rented. The landlady looks after the garden,' he said. It made sense. Seeing where he lived was like discovering another part of him.

He unlocked the door. I followed him in and took off my sandals. The terracotta floor tiles cooled my bare feet. The walls were white and fresh looking. The porch led into the sitting room, which faced directly onto the stairs. It had a low lintel, too small for Marc's height. I could tell just by looking that he must have hit his head on that lintel more than once. I smirked, envisioning the clonk to his head.

'Please, make yourself at 'ome,' he said, resting my bag down next to the stairs.

I sat down on his sofa. Then I bounced up and down.

'Comfy,' I said, turning to look at him.

What the hell was I doing? I stopped bouncing, like I was testing it out in a shop. I wasn't usually a performing monkey. I didn't usually display bizarre habits. But he was watching me. And I felt nervous, being in his lair. I drew a sharp intake of breath and promised myself I'd stop being weird. Acting completely normal was difficult.

'I'll get us the champagne,' he said.

As he walked off to the kitchen, I covered my face. *Oh God, he thinks I'm a freak.* Emma knew I was peculiar, but I'd hoped not to reveal that to Marc so soon. Moments later, he returned with two glasses and some chilled champagne.

'So 'ere we are. Thank you for coming,' he said and handed me a delicate flute.

'Thank you for having me,' I replied politely as we clinked glasses.

Shit. Had I really just said that? Thanks for having me was a phrase my Mum had drilled into me as a child, and it still obediently and automatically replayed each time polite behaviour was prompted. Trying to banish further thoughts, I forgave myself.

'I'm making chicken curry for dinner. I 'ope you like it?' he asked.

'I'm impressed.'

'Don't be too impressed. I'm sorry but I'm using a jar,' he said.

'If you hadn't have told me, I wouldn't have known,' I said, laughing.

It was an honest confession that surprised me because the French always seemed super proud of their cuisine.

'I 'ave plenty of time to impress you yet. We 'ave two days together. And 'ow am I doing so far?' he asked, with a cheeky grin.

'You've only just started, so you definitely need to keep trying,' I said, smiling.

'An 'ard woman to please,' he said with another smile.

He topped up our champagne. Marc was a good host. He soon put me at ease and I relaxed in his company, or maybe that was the champagne. I hadn't decided. Curling my legs up onto his sofa, I chilled out whilst he was in the kitchen.

When he emerged, he was carrying two plates of chicken curry. He walked past the sofa to the large, heavy looking table behind and placed them down.

'Dinner is ready. It doesn't look too good… but it tastes okay,' he said.

He seemed embarrassed by his efforts. And it wasn't the high self-assurance I'd have expected from a Frenchman delivering home-cooked cuisine, despite being assisted by a jar of commercial sauce. But I wasn't any better. In the Penthouse, the sound of the microwave ping was a regular occurrence. I kept that to myself.

He pulled out a chair for me at the table and beckoned me over. He seated me at his table. Inspecting the plate, it looked like chunks of chicken in an anaemic yellow sauce. But I couldn't have cared less.

'Looks good to me,' I said.

'Here, let me get you a glass of red. The French 'ave to 'ave wine before a meal,' he said.

Not only was he feeding me but attempting to educate me too. *Did he think I lacked awareness of French culture?* My knowledge wasn't extensive, but it wasn't completely non-existent.

'So, are you now trying to get me drunk on champagne *and* red wine?' I asked.

'Yes, of course,' he said with a huge smile.

I'd heard about Frenchmen having an in-bred knowledge of selecting wine for a meal – the Holy Trinity of French cuisine. Not that I knew anything about wine or cuisine, but I knew what I liked. And I liked him. He'd already lived up to his stereotypical talent for god-given sex appeal. He'd also been dealt more than his share of the romance genes at birth. And although he hadn't served up a culinary masterpiece, he was probably saving his best talent for dessert. Passion in abundance. The iconic art of seduction French style. I took a large gulp of champagne. *What did he think of me? Was I starchy and English?*

Pulling a cigarette lighter from his pocket, he lit a large white candle and moved it to the centre of the table. As he placed the lighter by the edge of his plate directly in my line of view, I was reminded again that he was a smoker. But I hadn't detected a smell of smoke on him or in his place. Not that I cared. Things were perfect.

Playing with my fork, poking at the curry on my plate before finally trying it, it was edible, but I still wasn't hungry. But as he'd gone to the trouble of cooking, I felt obliged to eat his offerings and managed to swallow small mouthfuls.

He touched the lighter with his fingers, making me wonder whether he had an urge and was accustomed to finishing off his meals with a smoke.

'So, how do you manage the running *and* smoking?' I teased.

He shrugged.

'Look, I like fine wine, good food and I enjoy smoking. I run because of the food and wine, but I'm not giving up the smoking. I like that too.' He smiled at me. 'I'm not giving any of that up just because it might not be good for me. Okay?' The *okay* was a statement, not a question. It was clear that he did as he pleased, confirming my suspicions about his stubbornness and *Darcy-esque* similarities.

We rounded off the meal draining the bottle of red. As the large round rim of my glass touched my face, I became vaguely aware of the potential for causing a stained expression. The type of look I accidentally achieved with lipstick, although usually confined to my mouth and teeth. But the combined effects of champagne and wine diluted my nerves and self-consciousness. And he was too polite to point out my lack of sophistication. Contentedly, I smiled.

He got up to tidy away the plates.

'Let me help,' I said.

'No. Please, you are my guest.'

And I really like being your guest, I whispered to myself before slurping the remains of my wine as he made his way towards the kitchen. When he returned, he gestured his hand towards the sofa, inviting me over. He collected our champagne glasses and set them down on the little glass coffee table in front. Then he sat next to me on the sofa, closer than before. The light flow of conversation had so far been general, but I wanted to concentrate a spotlight on him. And know *all* about him. I hardly knew anything.

'Seeing as you know about me, time to tell me about *your* hobbies,' I said.

'I like sailing. It's in my blood. I grew up with it as a young boy by the coast in France. I love the ocean. And you?' he asked.

'I've only done a bit. I learned to sail dinghies on a reservoir in England. Does that count?' I asked.

'Of course,' he said too chirpily, so I didn't believe him.

'Oh, and my granddad keeps a yacht in the Caribbean,' I said.

'You get to use it?' he said, his eyes sparkling when they looked at me. Whether it was his interest in me or the mention of the Caribbean sailing that was holding his attention, I couldn't decide.

'Only once, when he was in Italy, not the Caribbean. It was the holiday before I started university. I spent a week sailing around the coast of southern Italy when he was out that way. We travelled by car to Pisa and then got the train to La Spezia,' I said, purposefully leaving out the part about it being a terrible car journey. 'The views look amazing from a yacht. Watching the coastline was stunning. At night, I remember watching the glow of pretty red candles in the distance and poking my head through the porthole in my cabin to look at the coastline and stars in the sky... for hours. It was funny, sort of. But only afterwards. I arrived with this massive suitcase to take on his yacht.'

'No way,' he laughed.

'Yeah. Anyway, Sam, my evil and disgusting younger brother, thought it funnier to let me take it. That's brotherly love for you.'

'Disgusting brother?' Marc raised his eyebrows.

'Yes. He virtually lived in the clothes he went in and was more than happy to join the great unwashed the whole time we were there. He's disgusting like that,' I said.

'It's a bit like that with some sailing,' he said.

'I didn't mean that all sailors are revolting,' I added quickly, having remembered that some Frenchmen had a reputation for being a bit smelly. I hoped he didn't think that I was implying that he had a lack of hygiene. Silently, I cursed.

'And what 'appened to your case?' he asked.

'My granddad and brother tried to pull it on board. I had visions of watching my suitcase sink into the harbour after their first attempt failed, but fortunately my granddad came up with the sensible idea of unpacking some stuff to get it on board and make it lighter. Well, I hadn't realised that a suitcase wasn't appropriate for a boat, and if no one tells you, how are you supposed to know?' I asked.

'Of course.' He smiled at me. 'We'll get you a couple of smaller bags for my boat.'

'Excellent. I like shopping,' I said, whilst mentally noting the part about him mentioning us going to his boat, which would involve another date.

Telling stuff to Marc was easy. In a typed email, it wouldn't have been the same. It reminded me of wanting to tell him about flying over Corsica that time.

'I have to tell you about Italy; it's beautiful,' I said.

'Go on,' he said and nodded.

'The ocean is crystal clear by the coastline. There's all these delicate coloured fish that glisten in the sunlight. They layer the water in size, starting off tiny and getting bigger closer to the seabed. I'd never seen the bottom of the seabed until going to Italy, and I mean being quite a way out from the shore in a boat and the water being clear enough to see it all.' I had no idea if he was interested in what I was telling him, but when he continued to nod I interpreted it as positive.

'Amazing stuff,' he replied.

'We threw out an anchor and I swam in the sea, which I loved. When I climbed back on board, having survived climbing up the ladder with metal rungs – *which really hurt my feet* – then I got seasick. I lay down and tried to fix my gaze, which is what you're supposed to do, right?' I asked. He nodded. 'It must have been the sudden motion. According to my granddad, I had yet to find my sea legs.'

Oh God – did I just mention being seasick? I took a breath, and worried about having rambled on too much *and* the mention of vomit.

'I didn't even know there was a whole community out at sea either,' I said, thinking that further ramblings might help cover up the vomit.

'No?' said Marc, tilting his head to one side.

'People pass each other on boats and get to know each other, having moored together somewhere previously, or the ice-cream boats that look exactly the same on water as they do on land, minus the wheels, because it's a boat.' Marc laughed. I knew he was being polite, but I couldn't stop my verbal diarrhoea. 'Getting back on land was interesting. He had this dodgy old dinghy that you felt you risked your life in. He only spent money out of necessity.'

Marc laughed again then ran his fingers through his hair, the way I'd seen him do it before. He stretched out his arm on the seatback, grasping his glass of wine. He seemed so confident. He'd probably been everywhere and seen it all. Marc stroked his hair again and then stared at me intently, making me glance away, unable to meet his eyes at first. Then I looked back at him.

'Then there was one day when we watched a wedding procession through the ancient cobbled streets. I was eating lemon ice cream and wearing these cut-off scruffy shorts when this beautiful tanned Italian bride came by wearing a lace dress that trailed along behind her. It was just like watching a fairy tale romance of a wedding,' I said, unable to stop talking until I halted my babble, aware of having mentioned the words *fairytale*, *romance* and *wedding* all in the same sentence. The extent of my knowledge *or lack of* about sailing was exhausted.

There was a silent pause.

'Maybe I'll take you out to see him one day,' I said.

'Sure,' he said, shrugging his shoulders.

It seemed a completely realistic and viable idea in a quiet moment, and the right gesture at the time, although the fact that I'd only been once myself made it highly unlikely to happen.

He leant over me and topped up both our glasses. He was still an enigma; I hardly knew him. I'd banged on about myself too much.

'Tell me about you,' I said. 'What's the best thing about flying?'

He took a sip, then put his glass down on the table and turned to face me. 'The best thing about flying, umm... let me see. This might seem a bit, cheesy... I think that's the right word,' he said, looking at me for confirmation as I nodded and giggled. 'To fulfil a child'ood dream. Matter of fact, man's oldest dream. When I started working with light aircrafts it was the freedom of being alone, away from everything. Back then, there wasn't much restrictions to where you could go. Now with airliners, I don't know, everything is policed and run by investors.'

'That's a great cheesy answer,' I said, teasing him. But secretly I loved his answer, sharing a personal part of himself.

'You like that? Well, let me tell you my other dream: to live by the sea in a cottage filled with old furniture. Old furniture has a soul. It has lived and breathed a life before belonging to you,' he said.

His romantic vision sounded perfectly plausible coming from him. But I was a sucker for languages, charming their way into my heart. I'd never thought about furniture having a soul, but it was an interesting concept. Had an Englishman said it, I'm pretty sure that I would have choked on my champagne.

'My best piece is that table,' he said proudly, pointing over at where we'd eaten.

Anything he had to tell me was absorbing, like learning about his love of old wooden stuff. His voice was captivating. He made me smile. The similarity in his love of old things reminded me of Emma. Listening to him talk, the words he used, and the pitch and intonation of his voice was captivating.

'You like reading books?' he asked.

'Yes,' I shrugged, conscious of having imitated his mannerism. 'You?'

'Aeroplane manuals mainly. Just joking, although I 'ave to study them every six months for the Sim test. I read novels too, French ones, when I travel,' he said. 'Do you like the English Lakes? Looks beautiful flying over.'

'When you look up from your novel?' I joked. 'Actually, it's one of my favourite places. You talk about your cottage by the sea; well, I could happily live up in the Lakes… one day.'

'You know it?' he said, sounding surprised.

'Yeah. I've managed to visit a few places outside Birmingham Airport, you know.'

'Let's add that to our list of places to go together, along with visiting your granddad in the Caribbean,' he said, laughing. Then he glanced at his watch. 'It's late.'

Time felt irrelevant being with him. But time had escaped us, judging by the two bottles we'd slowly emptied together.

He finished off the last drop of his champagne. I sipped mine. He put down his glass and turned back towards me. Our eyes met. We smiled at each other. He reached out and carefully lifted my glass away. Then he stood up, offering out his hand for me. Placing my palm in his, slowly he pulled me to my feet. I trembled in anticipation. The alcohol had not entirely stemmed my nerves. Facing each other, he moved closer to me. Cupping my face in both his hands, tilting his head to one side, I felt his warm lips on mine. Then he kissed me again, tenderly and moved his hands to my waist, drawing me against his body. He slipped in his tongue and caressed my mouth. I pulled away unexpectedly. Then instinctively I threw myself back at him, responding to a sudden urge. He pressed his lips firmer to mine. My breathing quickened.

Things were yet unconsummated but there was an escalating, mutually requited feeling – a growing need. I wrapped my arms around his neck as he held me firmly against his body. I felt him rise. Then he picked me up in his arms and carried me over to the foot of the stairs. Placing me down, he grabbed my hand.

'Come on,' he said, leading me upstairs with a sense of urgency.

Standing by his bed, his hands travelled to my waist. He pulled me close and kissed me. A long, deep kiss.

The drink buzzed inside me as I reached a contented place of having lost my inhibitions but not so giddy as to lose full control. The mask of alcohol enabled a faux confidence as my hands ran over his body. My palms took in the sturdy feel of his chest beneath his smooth grey top. My fingers wandered, travelling further down, past his belt where my whole hand met with the bulbous feel of him pressing hard against the fabric of his jeans. Reaching for his belt buckle, I pulled it loose.

'Wait a minute,' he said.

Too far into the moment to protest or care, I sat on his bed, pulled off my top and unclasped the damned bra myself, discarding it on the floor and appreciating the release. I turned to see him standing by the foot of his bed and caught sight of him stripping off his blue boxers at lightning speed, flashing his bare arse. He dived under the dark covers and flipped back the duvet to reveal his naked body as he lay on his back. I crawled in naked and kneeled next to him. He lay there. I'd expected him to take control. I thought he would make a move, but he didn't. I stared down at him, puzzled by his flaccid dick.

Realising he needed resuscitation, I leant over him. My hair trailed his thighs as I took him in my mouth. He let out an unexpected moan. Surprised by his audible enjoyment, temporarily I stopped. His wide-eyed and open-mouthed look begged me to continue. I went back down enthusiastically and with my free hand I caressed his balls.

'Stop… stop,' he groaned.

I lifted my head from his groin. He stretched out his arm and pulled open his bedside drawer. He fumbled about, finally pulling out a packet. Then gripping it with his teeth, after a couple of attempts, he ripped it open. Holding the condom between his fingers, we both watched as he rolled it on.

'Guide me,' he said, offering me his now fully prepared stiff cock.

Inching forward on my knees, taking the lubricated feel of him in my hand, I pushed him inside, sinking my thighs down either side of his body. Rhythmically, I began taking him all in with each motion. Resting my hands on his chest, the up and down movement forced me to steady myself, realising that the effects of booze were not helping matters.

'Sorry, that's not very good,' I said, wanting to stop the bouncing.

'No. It's good… it's good,' he repeated.

I continued, but the awkwardness of the situation was becoming apparent, despite his encouragement.

'I'm sorry,' I said and brought all movement to a standstill.

'Turn over,' he said.

I climbed off him, feeling relief at the thought of getting to lie down on my back. He rose up on his knees and got behind me on the bed, taking hold of my hips. His grip was firm but gentle as he held me. Automatically, I leaned forward onto my hands, unexpectedly finding myself positioned like a dog on all fours. Releasing his grip, he slid his hand between my legs, rubbing me with his fingers. Wetness trailed down my inner thigh. I hoped he hadn't noticed the cellulite on the backs of my legs. I looked back as he wiped his hand against his own thigh. Then he placed both hands back around my waist and introduced his pelvis to my arse.

'Guide me,' he said.

Reaching behind, he felt limp again. Stuffing him back in place, he took over with a couple of quick thrusts before slowing to a gentle rhythm. It was more comfortable than before, being able to hold myself with my hands and him supporting me at the waist. He took one hand off my hips as he continued to thrust and smoothed his hand over my lower back, making me arch down as I relaxed. He leaned forward, penetrating deeper; his torso covered my body. I hoped it wouldn't take much longer. Pressed against me, he took hold of my boobs in his palms, preventing them jiggling as he pounded me faster and more vigorously with each thrust.

On hearing his euphoric moan, I felt his release like a fire extinguisher being squirted. Relieved at him having got there, the rocking sensation slowed. He collapsed down on the bed and slipped off the soggy-looking piece of rubber, dropping it beside the bed.

'Put your head on my shoulder,' he said, holding out his arms for me.

Tired and partially nauseous, I nestled into him; our bodies entangled with his arms wrapped around me. I couldn't keep my eyes open.

The next morning, I awoke to find him lying on his side, head in hand, staring across at me. Immediately, I pulled the covers over my body. Trying to hide, I felt awkward at being exposed in the sobering light of the morning sun peeping through the shutters, despite the actions of the previous night. And with smudged make-up, I was aware how awful my face looked in the morning. Instantly and sharply, he removed the covers from my body. He climbed on top. I wanted to escape. My teeth needed the once-over, but there was no chance. He trapped me. Sweeping my hair from my face, he kissed my lips.

He thoroughly studied my naked body, running his fingers the entire length of me. He whispered into my ear as his large hands stroked my mound. His French voice spilled seductive words about my soft and delicate English skin, acquainting himself with every inch of me; the same way he'd probably studied the controls of an aeroplane, but he was captain now. Having gained complete mastery, he pinned down my hands on the smooth sheets and pushed apart my legs with his knees. Then holding his position, he made me wait. On purpose.

Jet engines fired up and throttle engaged at the power setting, he thrust forward firmly. Powering along the runway, feeling the momentum of movement, he accelerated like Concorde. Engine temperatures in the take-off range, we became airborne, gliding upwards, cruising a while, prolonging the journey. Then on reaching altitude, an intense high voltage rush of electrical current ran through my body, before passing through his.

Easing off the throttle, reducing thrust and with a gradual decrease in motion, slowly and gently he descended. He brought all movement to a complete standstill, applying the brakes.

That was more like it and the way I'd thought about it in my head. He didn't disappoint, even though I wasn't rating his performance. And it was nothing like last night. The huge smile plastered on his face suggested he knew it too. I half expected him to light up a cigarette.

'I'll fix some breakfast,' he said with a lingering smile.

Then he combat-rolled out of bed. My eyes rested on the shapeliness of his bum as he strutted out of the bedroom door. I sprawled out in the stream of sunlight that filtered through the window. Giggling to myself, remembering that night in the Parisian bar – he said he'd teach me to fly. I hadn't contemplated it being quite so much fun. Gazing up at the ceiling and thinking more about his naked body, I hoped for another flying lesson.

Minutes later, he brought back coffee and croissants with honey on a tray. I'd been hoping to see him swing freely, but he'd thrown on some boxers and a t-shirt. It didn't matter. My imagination had already delivered. He was perfect – well, almost. Marc had some learning to do. He brought me coffee not tea, but as he'd already scored highly for delivering breakfast in bed, I forgave him.

'Today, we'll go for a drive. I'll take you past Chantilly Forest. Then we can head to the Palace of Versailles. You like that?' he asked.

'Sounds good,' I said, not bothered in the slightest and thinking it was bound to involve some king called Louis. All French history seemed to involve a Louis of some description.

I didn't care what we did. My head was still in a fuzzy, yet happy place. And content just to be with him, Paris was a bonus. The whole exploring France thing had passed me by in my excitement to arrive. It amused me that Marc now had the impression that I was into cultural stuff. Although I couldn't remember everything we'd discussed from last night, I could clearly picture what had followed.

'Don't you want any of these croissants?' I asked.

'Café,' he replied, holding up his cup. I'd forgotten that he wasn't a breakfast man. 'I'll go shower, you take your time,' he said, leaving me to feast on his tray of delights.

He kissed me on the cheek and grabbed a towel from the back of his door, flinging it over his shoulder. Lifting the tray to one side, I swung out of bed with his duvet wrapped around me. Scooping back the curtain, I peeped through the window. The sun shone. It looked to be another fantastic, carefree and roasting hot summer's day in Paris. My white floaty dress would be just right.

Trying to look pretty, it took time alternating between the bathroom mirror and the one in his bedroom. The bathroom light was better for fiddling with make-up application. And the mirror sat on the shelf above the sink, positioned at just the right height for me. He'd have to bow over it for shaving. In his bedroom, the larger oak-framed mirror on the wall above the set of drawers was bigger and better for fixing my hair. I'd avoided wetting it in the shower, trying to retain the waves from yesterday. Pushing my fingers through the roots, I lifted and sprayed with *firm hold*, adding more volume. My hair fell nicely over my shoulders.

In the kitchen, Marc attempted to top up my coffee.

'*Non, merci,*' I said.

Placing my hand over the top of my mug, politely I refused the refill. Then I pulled out a freezer bag from my dress pocket and produced a teabag. He stood and watched, still with the coffee pot in one hand.

'Where's your kettle?' I asked, looking around the worktop surfaces, but not able to spot it.

'What kettle? You English people 'ave kettles. We 'ave coffee machines. I can't believe you brought your own teabags,' he laughed.

'I guessed that you wouldn't have any... and I was right.'

'You can boil some water in a pan if you like... or drink some café. We'll make a good Frenchwoman out of you yet,' he said.

'In the meantime, I'm still English and I like tea,' I replied.

He put a pan of water on to boil whilst I contemplated how different we were – the French and the English. The French were only across the Channel. A kettle was much more practical than boiling a pan of water. He obviously didn't know many tea-drinking English people.

After knocking back my tea like a coffee addict, we headed out.

'I'm sorry about the air conditioning not working. It stopped working only a few days ago,' he said. His car was burning hot.

'Don't worry; I'm enjoying the breeze,' I lied.

I hoped that my hair wouldn't resemble that *just-out-of-bed look* by the time we arrived. The forceful gust that hit me from the side prompted me to rummage through my bag for a spare hair tie. Flipping up the vanity mirror, I assembled my hair into a loose ponytail, more casual than the scraped-back bun I wore for work.

The heat of the sun beating through was intense, making it a warm and sticky ride, even with the windows down. As a last-minute thing, I'd chucked some deodorant into my bag. I was pleased about that now, even though it made my bag bulkier. Keeping my arms spaced apart from my body avoided sweat patches, although it forced me to adopt a rigid pose.

'You okay?' he shouted, over the noisy hum of traffic.

'Yep. Fine, thanks.'

He didn't realise the inconvenience of his air conditioning having packed up. The effort of getting ready was probably off his radar – something reserved for the female of the species and a triviality to him. He just ran his fingers through his hair to put it all back in place.

'The tree-lined road is Chantilly Forest; it goes further back,' he said.

'Looks pretty.'

On any other occasion, I would have loved him showing me his France. But being blasted in a wind tunnel and baked in a fan oven whilst trying to avoid a dishevelled appearance was putting me off the scenic route.

'We'll picnic there at some point,' he said.

Today would have been ideal. I smiled back and kept quiet, not wanting to spoil his plans. Walking hand-in-hand through a forest had more appeal than coping with the hordes of tourists that were bound to face us at the Palace of Versailles.

We queued to get in. Standing behind Marc, I was aware of his body acting as a shelter when the wind blew. Following Marc inside, I noticed his slight swagger and since he'd removed his wallet, how his jeans curved the rocks of his bum, reminding me how he looked good *sans* jeans too. Then he turned around, handing me a guide. Tactfully, I skimmed the English section. The mention of King Louis privately amused me.

It was crowded as expected, but I was used to being huddled in with passengers on planes, although this place held far more people. As we shuffled along, herded through rooms, I looked up occasionally at the gold ornate objects. But I paid greater attention to looking down at the chequered black and white tiles, trying not to step on toes, until Marc took hold of my hand. I focussed on his warm, firm grip. That was more like it. A butterfly sensation re-emerged.

'Come on. I show you the 'All of Mirrors. It's most famous,' he said.

As he led me away, I didn't care where we were going. Amongst the crowd of people and the babble of low-speaking voices, he stopped and let go of my hand. Stepping behind me, he directed my body towards the centre of the room. His hands guided my hips.

'So. What do you think?' he asked.

The reflective rows of giant blingy chandeliers on display weren't any match for the tingling sensation trickling down my neck with every breath of his caressing my skin.

'Impressive,' I whispered.

'Come on… let's get out of 'ere.'

As he spoke, the tone of his voice echoed through my body. Turning to face him, his soft lips touched mine, but only briefly. It was too public for more.

Pleased that he'd caught my vibe about heading out, we made for the centre of Paris by car. The busy traffic-filled streets on a Monday afternoon made Paris seem alive. Parisians liked using car horns.

'Have you climbed the Tour d'Eiffel?' he asked, looking over at me whilst driving.

'Yeh,' I replied. He needn't know that I was thirteen and on a school trip at the time.

'Good. I don't 'ave to climb all those steps with you then. I've been up there many times… unless you want?' he asked.

'Maybe another time.'

Was that his usual choice of outing for romantic liaisons with lovers? Dropping the thought, I let it go and restrained myself from asking. Then as we drove by, he pointed out the Arc de Triomphe.

'The roads join at a point to form a star shape,' he said. Vaguely, I recalled the name from the same high school trip. Marc was still trying to educate me on the topic of France. It was kind of cute. 'We'll take a walk along the Champs Elysees. You can tour the shops.'

Now he was talking my language – shopping trips. The exclusive and high-end Parisian shops were out of my league in terms of the contents of my purse, but I could window-shop. Eyeing up luxury goods was more my style, rather than a culture or history lesson. Not that I didn't have an appreciation, but with a hot man in Paris there were better things to do.

We parked in an underground car park.

'Take a look round the shops, and when you're finished, we'll do lunch. Go wherever you like. Are you 'appy with that?' he asked.

'More than okay,' I said.

Was he a man that liked shopping? Thrilled with his suggestion, I doubted it was his thing, having never met a man, other than Henri, that liked to shop.

We strolled down the bustling street. I spotted Louis Vuitton. Then a wicked idea occurred.

'Let's go here first,' I said, pointing to the shop.

Dragging him by the hand, I couldn't help responding to a devilish urge. How far would he be prepared to go to make me happy? We walked in. The shop assistant muttered some French words.

'I'm English,' I said, almost apologetically.

The sparsity of the shop meant that everything was immaculate and had its place. Marc stood by the door whilst I checked out the displays of bank-draining bags on offer. I'd never stepped inside a genuinely posh handbag store before, other than airport ones. My eyes rested on a swish-looking piece displayed on a stand. Not knowing whether I could touch it without first asking, I plucked it from the stand by its thick brown leather straps and ruined their neat display. The assistant watched. I didn't bother to read the price tag; I knew it was massively beyond my means. I studied its features, examined the pockets and stroked my fingers over the heritage golden brass hardware.

'Marc, do you have your credit card on you?' I said, turning to him.

Marc stalled for a minute.

'Uhh… sure,' he said. His face lacked expression.

I held out my hand.

'You don't mind, do you?' I asked.

He looked at me, perplexed, until a serious look caught up with his thinking. Then I could tell he was uncomfortable. He reached for his wallet in his back pocket; even though he'd told me all about the pickpockets, still he kept it there. Holding the bag in one hand and waiting for him to hand me his card with the other, I could see the raised eyebrow of the sales assistant taking more than an interest. Marc drew a card from his wallet. Stalling, he held it in his hand, until he outstretched his arm to pass it to me.

'Actually, I've changed my mind. I'll have a think about it. There's another one I want to look at first,' I said.

I put down the bag on the counter, grabbed Marc's hand and waltzed out of the shop. Then I burst out laughing.

'I just wanted to see if you would,' I teased him.

'What! You nearly gave me an 'eart attack,' Marc said, coming to terms with the prank. 'Did you see the price tag on that thing?'

'Nope.'

He lit up a cigarette.

''Ow do they say…there's another side to you, I think.'

'Oh yes. We're just getting to know each other. Let's skip the shops and move on to lunch. How about it?' I said.

'Gladly. My card can 'andle that,' he said.

After a short stroll, and time for him to finish his cigarette, we found a little pizza place tucked away down a back street, *alfresco* style. We sat down at a table and a well-dressed waiter brought out a couple of menus.

'Do you need me to 'elp you with the menu?' he asked.

'I'll go for *pizza margherite* and a Perrier, s'il vous plait,' I proudly replied, not wanting to appear too ignorant. It was the only pizza I knew in French.

Sitting opposite our table was another young couple – a pretty blonde with her boyfriend. I assumed that's who he was because of the mild bickering. He'd just paid the bill and was trying to leave a tip. Although I didn't understand the conversation, he'd placed some copper coins on the table. She made him take them away by pushing them aside in favour of silver coins. He did exactly as she instructed. I picked all this up without understanding a word. Curious, I asked Marc, 'Would you leave copper coins for a tip?'

He'd been oblivious to the goings-on with the other couple. He looked at me bizarrely.

'They 'ave to make a living, so it's not a good idea.' He shrugged.

I liked his answer. The girl had been instantly obeyed by the guy, which got me thinking about relationships between men and women in France. *How different was their culture?* I thought back to the handbag prank – poor Marc. He would have gone through with it, I felt sure. Maybe that's why Marc had been prepared to hand me his credit card and not protest at my attempt to become a gold-digger. I could have taken full advantage. He wasn't stupid, though. He'd have dumped me afterwards. I giggled.

'What's the joke this time?' he asked.

'Just thinking back to earlier. Planning your next heart attack,' I said.

'I'm going to 'ave to watch out,' he said with a grin.

Our pizzas arrived. They could have fed us twice over. My food disorder (the one where I couldn't eat around him) had vanished. Despite being starving, my pizza was the size of a serving plate. But there was no way I could eat it all. I usually shared one the same size with Emma, even though this one had a thin, crispy crust. Plus I didn't want to end up bloated, even though I wasn't wearing slim jeans. Stuffing myself usually resulted in undoing my top button, enabling a muffin-top hangover, but cleverly disguised by my jacket. Today, my pretty dress would adequately float over any incidents. But there was potential to look very unattractive in pants later. I left half. I couldn't hide bloating stood in knickers.

After lunch, we ambled along the streets together in the sun, with no purpose in particular, but soaking up the sights and sounds of Paris. And the feeling of bliss was complete, having a Frenchman by my side. He took hold of my hand and led me to some nearby gardens within a park. Swiss Valley Gardens were almost secluded from the rest of Paris, but ironically just a stroll away from the Champs Elysees; a contrast to the hubbub of the city. We found a spot on the grass, away from the rest of Paris, and lay down in the sun, looking up at the sky.

Dreamily, I watched the floating clouds drift by. It was a perfect summer romance in the capital of love. Perhaps, to any onlookers, we were a passionate French couple that met up during their lunch breaks and bonked like mad before returning to the office, flustered. I liked the fantasy.

'My eardrums are still giving me trouble. I 'ave a doctor's appointment later today. We better get going,' Marc said.

He interrupted my fantasy bubble of a moment. But I forgave him, even though he was unaware of the gesture. He'd been suffering with his ears. I knew that. And it was partly the reason I was there. He'd done well not to moan about it. But it now seemed an inconvenience rather than an excuse to see each other.

It was late afternoon and we were back at his place. I said I'd do my yoga whilst he was out.

'I could stay and watch,' he suggested with a cheeky grin.

'Get to the doctor's. I'll show you some *yoga* later.'

'If you promise.'

He got down on the floor to where I was sitting on a makeshift mat, having improvised with one of his towels. He delivered a lengthy kiss. The type where you end up glued to each other, not wanting to come unstuck. It nearly resulted in another flying lesson, but we resisted.

'You made me a promise for later,' he said. His eyes flashed as he got up to leave.

'Don't be long,' I replied.

Hearing his car engine grow fainter as he drove off, I was alone, and in his place. A perfect opportunity to get to know Marc a bit better, despite him not being there. Starting with his passport on the sideboard, I checked through his details. His photo aged him, but pictures in passports were never complimentary. And it wasn't about his looks. His date of birth confirmed his age, not that I suspected he'd lied or that I even noticed our age gap. But his confidence made him attractive. Closing his passport shut, I put it back in the same spot and headed upstairs.

His wardrobe door creaked as it opened. Uniform filled the left side with shirts and jumpers on the right. Apart from a navy jumper, he wore a lot of black and grey. His leather jacket hung at the end. He wore it to work over his uniform, in colder weather. Running my hand across it, I let my fingers explore the silky feel of the inside.

Yoga Tantrics

Coming up into *cobra*, I knew I should have given it more time after the pizza lunch. It was confirmed when going into a *downward dog*. Instantly I felt queasy. Cutting the session short, I skipped to the meditative part.

It reminded me of the time I'd felt sick when flying on the *Dash*. Only this time I wasn't suspended in the air at thirty thousand feet, mercilessly strapped into a crew seat and about to be devastatingly embarrassed. No way would I ever share that detail with Marc, even though Emma had found it hilarious.

The end was always the best bit. Lying on the floor in the darkness with an empty head, allowing complete inner peace to wash over me. I loved it, a bit like rolling over contentedly after having experienced the best sexual climax, which hadn't happened often… until recently.

I fetched a glass of water and sat on the sofa to let the nauseous feeling pass. Having recovered from the *downward dog*, I looked through his collection of CDs stacked next to the TV. Nothing was familiar. Maybe I'd listen later. I picked up the remote control for the TV, not expecting to be able to work it. When it burst into life at the click of a red button, I surpassed my own expectations. Flipping through the channels, I paused at a kids' cartoon. Trying to decipher the French, I sprawled back on his sofa, distracted with teaching myself some phrases, including *le singe mange des bananes* (the monkey eats bananas).

The next minute, I heard Marc's car pull up outside. I hadn't realised how long I must have spent watching TV. A nervous thrill ran through my body as I wondered whether I should meet him at the door. Instead, I switched off the TV and in a stupid sense of urgency, I ran to the shower upstairs. Having rolled around on the floor, I wanted to freshen up. It was the fastest shower as the water barely touched my skin. By the time he came through the front door, I was virtually getting dry. Hearing his footsteps getting closer on the stairs made me tremble excitedly.

'Get dressed; I'm taking you out for dinner,' he said as I opened the bathroom door and he stood smiling at me on the landing.

Temporarily blocking me from entering his bedroom, he looked me up and down, still smiling. Instinctively, I pulled my towel tight to my body and looked down at the floor. *Why was I so shy and prudish?*

Knowing he'd locked the bathroom door, when I walked into his bedroom, I threw off my towel on his bed and shouted, 'Somewhere fancy, I hope.'

'Put on a nice dress, I want to show you off at my favourite restaurant,' he said with the bathroom door still shut.

Secretly, I squealed at the thought of a fancy restaurant. Nobody had ever taken me to experience their *favourite* restaurant. And definitely not *to show me off*. It made me wish I'd taken more time in the shower. My hair needed washing. An up-do was my best bet, with a few loose strands.

I wanted to look pretty for him. I dug out the fitted little black number I had with me, courtesy of Emma. She'd thrown it in last minute as a *just in case*, along with the *dobbers*. Later, I'd text her to say thanks. I'd had about three texts from her that day wanting all the gossip. Her latest one read: *How was ur adult sleepover? Hope u used dobbers.* It was mainly nosiness but also her way of showing she cared. I hadn't yet replied.

Marc had showered and changed. It was the first time I'd seen him dressed up, complete with his leather jacket. It had got chillier now it was evening. His swept-back hair and unshaven look suited him. He looked proper hot wearing a dark shirt and smart jeans. His jeans clung to him where it counted. His aftershave filled my lungs as he drew me close for a kiss. One of his hands rested on my lower back, just high enough that he touched my skin exposed through the deep-cut "V" on the reverse of my dress. A tingly shiver ran through me. Wanting to jump him then and there, I exercised self-control, although I wasn't sure why. He'd already had me.

'You look amazing,' he said, speaking softly into my ear. I felt myself blush. 'I'm taking you somewhere special. It 'as a balcony outside where we can sit if you like and a pianist in the bar. You came all this way just to see me. I 'ope you like it.'

'Well, it's been quite a hardship but I can put up with you a bit longer, if I must,' I said with a smile, then added a shoulder shrug.

'We can start with champagne cocktails. It's pretty special,' he said.

'Okay. I'll let you try and impress me.'

He drove us to a place in the suburbs. It was that hazy time of evening before darkness but when the light is starting to disappear. The restaurant was lit up with rows of tiny fairy lights and hanging lanterns. We were welcomed in and shown straight to a table outside on a balcony, just as he'd described. And the type of place where you hoped you knew which piece of cutlery to use. All I could remember was to start from the outside and work in, but I'd take my lead from Marc. The doors were pushed open to the main seating area, and inside was a pianist playing soft melodic jazz. Our table was private. There were a few other couples, but it wasn't busy – empty, as expected for a Monday.

'You wouldn't expect a pianist on a Monday,' I said.

'You're in Paris,' he said, then added, 'I 'ave a confession. 'E's a friend of mine – a buddy. Not the owner, just the pianist. I'm working on the owner – becoming a buddy, I mean. So, my friend plays 'ere at weekends. Sometimes 'e comes just to practise. I asked for 'im to come 'ere tonight.'

'Wow,' I replied, stumped for anything further to say.

'You're a beautiful woman,' he said, touching my knee with his hand under the table.

'Thank you,' I said, almost bursting into laughter. He made me glow. I wondered whether all Frenchmen were born with an innate ability for romance, or whether it was a learned art. Whatever it was, Englishmen needed lessons.

The champagne cocktails arrived. They were large and fancy-looking with an arrangement of thin fruit and crushed ice on top. I took a sip. The sweet taste made me lick my lips.

'If you don't mind, I'm going to order for you – if you'll let me, that is? I don't usually do that, but I want you to try what I think is the best they 'ave on the menu. That okay?' he asked.

Upmarket style seduction was not something I was familiar with. His offer was right on cue seeing as my brain had turned to mush, making it impossible for me to decipher a menu. Maybe this was what older men did, or older foreign men.

'Perfect,' I said. I hoped it would be. It wasn't that long since we'd eaten an enormous pizza, even if I had only eaten half. Keeping in mind that posh places rarely did big portions, I was bound to be okay. 'And what is the best they have?'

'Seabass. *C'est magnifique*,' he said, kissing his fingers. 'The dish is cooked to perfection. You 'ave to try it.'

'Okay,' I replied, smiling, whilst my face hid what I secretly detested.

A fish fan I was not. And the thought of fish served complete with a face violated my appetite. It made my stomach lurch. I preferred my fish *Captain Birdseye* style – in a finger, unidentified and smothered in tomato sauce. But it seemed a better idea to hide that revelation for now and bury thoughts of fish.

'So, you've been on your best behaviour, so far,' I said, whilst running my finger around the rim of my glass to try and help me concentrate. The cocktail wasn't helping matters; tasting good but obviously potent. 'I haven't seen much in the way of flaws.'

'Flaws?' he asked.

'You know, tell me what your faults are,' I said, leaning in, trying not to drool.

'Oh. Why would I want to do that?' He shrugged. 'You might run away! Why don't you tell me yours?'

'I can't believe you're asking me that question. I don't have any,' I said.

'Same,' he said. 'You only get to know that when you know each other well, don't you think? I've got my faults, not too many, or flaws as you call them – in the past. For instance, when I was eighteen, I 'ad a girlfriend. It was a long-distance thing. She was my first real relationship. I don't think either of us were faithful. She definitely wasn't. But that was a long time ago. I was stupid then. It didn't work out, as you'd expect. But I learned my lesson. I don't know whether she did. But I've never done anything like that since.'

His eyes caught mine. His big, dark intense eyes stared at me and his smile lit up his face.

'More champagne?' he asked and called the waiter over without waiting for my reply. I hadn't yet finished the first. It was my last chance to tell him about fish as he placed our order. But not wanting to spoil things, I let it go. I'd tell him another time, when he wasn't trying so hard to impress. And there was plenty of booze to wash it down.

'You're not getting me drunk again.' I laughed, thinking I'd better save a full glass.

'But it's more fun,' he replied cheekily. 'Sorry, I forgot to ask 'ow your yoga was earlier. You were going to show me, remember?'

'I don't remember saying that exactly. But the yoga was good, thank you. I didn't do much, actually. I think that pizza we had at lunchtime didn't agree with yoga. I didn't feel good. I hadn't felt like that since flying on the *Dash* a few months ago,' I said, without thinking.

'Wait a minute. So that *was* you?' he said.

'Was me what?' I asked.

'I 'eard about what happened on the *Dash*, but I didn't believe it was you,' he said.

Shit. How did he even know about that? And why the hell had I just mentioned it? Unable to lift my eyes to meet his, I sat there not knowing what to say next. And that if *he* knew, then probably *everyone* knew about it. He was probably picturing me yacking up all over the aircraft and finding me revolting along with his dinner. I wanted to slope off in shame.

'Don't worry. It's 'appened to me too. But I don't think I made such a good job,' he said, laughing.

I didn't believe him, but I raised my reddened face as he continued laughing, then masked my face with my hands.

'It was really embarrassing,' I replied, suddenly finding it amusing too. 'In front of all those passengers. I'm still mortified about that.' Peeping through my fingers, I checked whether he was still entertained or appalled.

'Sure,' he nodded, with a huge grin.

'Who told you?' I asked.

'Ron. We 'ad a night-stop. But 'e's forgetful with names so I thought 'e got confused. I couldn't imagine...' he said then paused. *Bloody Ron.* Not wanting Marc to continue any further, I interrupted.

'Now, I want to know about you. Tell me about running the Paris marathon,' I asked, keen to skip over the subject of vomit, fast, and before food arrived.

'What's to tell? I ran it. It was something I wanted to do. I like the freedom of running. I show you tomorrow,' he said as a matter of fact.

'Okay,' I replied, thinking nothing more of it.

'But my real passion, the thing I love, and I think you know this now... is sailing. But I'm afraid we'll run out of time before I can show you that... this time,' he said.

'You mean there'll have to be a next time?' I asked. As we smiled at each other across the table, my body smouldered in warmth at the thought of him wanting to see me again.

'I 'ope so,' he said.

The food arrived. A purple beetroot dish with salad leaves and dotted with sauce. The fish course was still to come, a couple of dishes in.

He told me more about learning to sail as a child, having been taught by his dad, and how he'd grown up with it being a part of him. He mentioned the special part of France by the coast that he kept returning to. I couldn't help but soak up his every word. His background fascinated me. He spoke of his interests with passionate enthusiasm and oozed natural charm.

'You can show me next time,' I said.

'Definitely,' he said, nodding his head. He reached out his hand and placed it on mine, looking into my eyes. 'And, you're coming to my party, right?'

'Yes. I'll just need to look into hotels for that,' I said. The words had dribbled starchily from my mouth, making me feel prudishly English.

'You're not staying at no 'otel. You're staying with *me*. That's settled,' he said.

'Okay then,' I laughed, but his intentions were clear.

It made me determined to swallow anything put on my plate, fish-face included.

Arriving back at his, Marc fixed us some drinks. Remembering his music collection from earlier and curious about his taste, I ran my fingers down his CDs. Randomly selecting one, I inserted it into his stereo and pushed play. A soft-sounding jazz rhythm made me sway. I began humming the tune, and as I turned, Marc was watching. I stopped. But taking my hands in his, he placed them over his shoulders. He grasped my waist and as his hips pressed close to mine, he started to rock me gently. Our feet shuffled in time to the music.

I kicked off my stilettos. He kissed me then swept me up, putting me down on his sofa. We kissed again. His fingers encroached on my thigh as he ran a hand under the fabric of my dress, reaching my knickers. His fingers lingered. My heart pumped faster. Then he grabbed my hand and pulled me to my feet. I was so wet I thought I'd collapse.

'Come on. I can't do what I want to do to you 'ere,' he said.

'Okay,' I whispered, biting my lip.

'Let me show you,' he said.

He pulled me into his arms and we tumbled onto his bed. Then his eyes locked on mine. His hand reached beneath my dress and parted my legs. His fingers travelled up between my legs until he reached my knickers. He swept aside the damp patch and with a single finger, he stroked beneath. I closed my eyes. Then removing his hand, he climbed on top. He lowered my knickers to my knees then worked the slither of fabric all the way down to my ankles. He rolled me over. Face down, I felt my zip come free. His hand slid under my bra. Nudging aside the loose straps, he pushed his palms upwards, fondling my breasts from beneath. Turning me back to face him, his pupils were wide. He tugged at the front of my dress, fully exposing my breasts. He moved his hand up my thigh and rubbed at my crotch. Then I yanked at his belt with unhinged desire and reached inside, feeling the stiffness of his arousal. The more I kneaded him, the heavier his breathing became, until he grasped my legs and pushed apart my thighs. Hoisting me over his arms, he drew me towards him. His head burrowed between my legs. I tried to hold back. But as his tongue flicked the spot, an uncontrollable moan escaped.

The next morning arrived too quickly.

'Wake up,' said Marc.

My head was tucked under a pillow, but I could hear the faint sound of his voice. I'd pulled the pillow over my head to block out the brightness of the morning light.

'You brought your training shoes, right?' he asked. His voice was barely audible.

'My trainers?' I said, just about forcing some words from my mouth.

'Good. You want to go running? It's sunny. Let's get out there. Right away,' he said.

'Today… like now?' I croaked.

Why had I said I wanted to run a marathon? It was a stupid ambition that needed abandoning. *Where were the croissants and hot tea?* I'd have settled for coffee, followed by another steamy sack session. My hands scrabbled around the wooden floor for my mobile. The screen glared 7 am. Ridiculous o'clock. Yoga didn't even happen that early. And I enjoyed that.

'Come on. You'll have fun. Meet me downstairs when you're dressed,' he said.

Fun? Who's he fucking kidding? I peeled the pillow off my face. There was no point faking enthusiasm; it was betrayed by my facial expression.

He stuck his lips on mine. It caught me by surprise. *Had he noticed my disgusting morning breath?* The breath sniff test wasn't necessary. I blamed the fish from last night. Launching myself back down on the bed, I failed to find his enthusiasm catching.

Having only brought one workout outfit, I put on yesterday's pink shorts and black t-shirt and dowsed myself in deodorant. Burying my nose into my armpit, there was no *honk of BO*. I grabbed my trainers and headed downstairs. Marc's hand gripped the back of the sofa. His head was visible over the top. He performed on-the-spot lunges, hands on hips, wearing the tightest shorts, which left nothing for my imagination. *Who'd kidnapped my sexy Frenchman and replaced him with an over-zealous stick-legged action man?* The shorts seemed capable of a chaffing incident, but I'd only ever heard of runner's nipple. Attempting to disguise a chuckle, I coughed then pretended to wipe my nose.

'Got to warm up properly,' he said, with a look of concentration and seriousness on his face. I had no intention of making a tit of myself. I burst out laughing. 'Oh, you think this is funny?' he said, with a grin. The he waffled on about tight muscles or something, whilst slapping the backs of his thighs, adding to his ridiculousness.

'Just enjoying the view,' I said, although I much preferred the Adonis from last night.

He opened the front door.

'Let's go. Just a gentle jog to start with,' he said.

'To start with!' I repeated.

After a couple of minutes of exertion, and a good part-way down the street, he started doing a backwards jog and watched me.

'Okay. I want to be positive for you... but you look like a distressed Bambi,' he told me firmly. 'Drop your shoulders. Just relax. It's a beautiful day... enjoy.'

'I didn't know you expected me to look good doing this.' I panted, felt self-conscious and tried to retain a level of dignity.

It took roughly five minutes to run around the block. He was a few steps ahead. But I managed to muster the effort to raise my voice and get him to stop.

'I'm done,' I said. Disappointed in myself and yoga for not being better at running, I wouldn't admit it to him.

'Okay.' He reached inside his shorts. ''Ere's the key.' He pulled out a cord with his key attached at the end. I watched. As it dangled, he untied the knot. Then he reached out and placed it in the palm of my hand. 'Let yourself in; meet you back at my place in about 'alf an 'our.'

The key was warm, but not sweaty. And too knackered and out of breath to care, I couldn't fathom whether it was gross or kinky.

'Half an hour?' I wheezed.

'Gonna get a few miles in. Do your yoga. We'll do brunch when I'm back,' he said, then took off at speed.

Surely, he wasn't going to do that much when he had an ear problem? He was probably stubborn and foolish. As he ran, he kept tapping the side of his head, so I knew it was an irritation.

Having taken time to recover on the sofa with a glass of water, I stared at the walls, noticing the sparsity of pictures. Being rented probably explained it. My attention was drawn to a massive sailing picture on his wall close to the window. The strong colours drew me closer to look at it. To the far side was his piano. He'd said he could play by ear. I wondered how good a musician he was. A few framed photos sat on top. On closer inspection, I guessed they were family members, apart from the one of a great big, long-haired dark dog. Extracting it, the happy, dewy-eyed and big toothed expression reminded me how people said owners looked like their dogs, although it couldn't be a recent pet. He was never around to take care of it. I wouldn't ask if it had died. Putting it back in place, as I moved away, I bumped my leg into the corner of a set of drawers next to the piano.

'Bugger!' I shouted.

Frantically, I reached down and rubbed my leg, trying to relieve the throbbing pain. One of the drawers hadn't been closed properly. There was a piece of paper poking out. I pulled it out. Logic and privacy escaped me in the moment. The content was typed in English.

It concerned a job offer – a captain's position based in Indonesia. I re-read it. Checking the date, it was only a few days old. It was surely one of the most dangerous places to fly. Stuffing the letter back in the drawer exactly as I'd found it, drawer still partially open, my thoughts raced. *Had he accepted? Was he going to tell me? If so, why was I here – a weekend shag?*

There was a knock on the frosted window panel of the door. He was back. My heart beat faster. My brain must have conveyed a puzzled look to my face.

'You okay?' he said, panting and slightly out of breath.

'Yes, fine. I'll get you some water,' I said.

Pleased to exit the room, the excuse was time to compose myself. I took a breath and filled a glass with water. Things had been too good to be true. When I returned, he was half naked. He mopped his head with his already sweat-drenched top. A few drips landed on the floor.

I fixed that image in my mind. It was foul, and referral material if I needed to get over him.

'Listen, I'll take a shower and we'll fix up some brunch. Sound good?' he asked.

'I'll be right here,' I said.

'What time did you say your flight was?' he asked.

'12.25,' I replied.

'Okay, we still got time,' he said as he ran upstairs.

Time for what? Time for a chat? Time to tell me he'd enjoyed his shaggathon and now he was fucking off to Indonesia?

A sinking feeling groaned in the pit of my stomach as I tried to analyse my thoughts. If I hadn't discovered the letter, then everything would have been just fine… which wasn't true. The evidence was lying in a drawer behind me. There was no way he'd knock back the opportunity.

Marc came downstairs.

'You like omelette?' he asked.

'Yeah, that's fine,' I said, trying to smile.

'Come with me,' he said, and pecked me on the cheek as we went into the kitchen. I turned my head. He paused but didn't say anything.

He took out pots and pans and laid out eggs and tomato and basil from the fridge.

'Am I getting a lesson?' I asked, trying not to sound sarcastic.

'This is omelette-making French style,' he said, delighting in his culinary skills. 'The secret is in the mixing. It's lighter this way,' he said, almost as though he were sharing a top secret. He handed me the jug. 'Keep going.' I copied his whisking until my arm was about to drop off. He added tomato and loads of basil.

We sat down at his French table again. He served our omelettes. I tasted it. There was no wine this time and no music or candles either. He was due to deliver me back to the airport. My stuff still needed to be packed. Not that it would take long. I'd throw it back in the case.

'Do you like it?' he asked.

'It's fine,' I replied.

'Come on. It's better than just fine. It's good, don't you think? And now you know how to make it, French style,' he said.

'Yes, I do,' I replied.

We ate our lunch quietly, catching glimpses of each other with an occasional smile as we looked up from our plates. The letter had stolen my concentration. It acted as a silent barrier to prevent the flow of conversation. But our time together was draining fast. Neither one of us had yet broached the subject about seeing each other again, apart from the mention of his party.

A Goodbye Kiss

My clothes lay scattered about his room. Momentarily pausing to remember last night and committing it to memory, I gathered up my stuff and shoved everything into my suitcase before heading back downstairs.

Standing at the open window overlooking the courtyard, he looked so tall with his back to me. From where I sat, not quite within reaching distance of him, he almost blotted out the light on one side of the window, the rustic shutters cast wide apart as he leaned forward. Resting his elbows on the windowsill, he blew out wisps of smoke. A gentle, warm summer breeze filled the air and slightly ruffled strands of his dark hair. Turning his head to glimpse over his shoulder at me, our eyes met briefly before I diverted mine to the canvas picture on his wall.

'Beautiful, isn't it?' he said, between the puffs of smoke from his cigarette, which curled off into the distance.

Hearing the intonation of his voice still made me melt. The way he spoke English in such a romantic French accent. In my heart, I couldn't help it; my feelings for him were more than fondness.

'Perfect,' I replied.

'I love the ocean. Best place on Earth.'

He was unaware that my attention was directly on him. Or if he was, he was diverting it as the realisation struck me that he was talking about the unmissable large canvas, the same one I'd looked at earlier, rather than the view from his window. The stark contrasting colours forced you to acknowledge it. A huge dark blue ocean scene dotted with fishing boats and a deep orange sunset on the horizon. I pondered; if he hadn't become an airline pilot, he would most certainly have been skippering a boat. Both pursuits were his passion.

He drew a few more drags on his cigarette, before turning around and pulling out a chair with his free hand, sitting down to face me at the table. His cigarette still occupied his fingers. It was the same spot where only a couple of nights previously we'd sat cosily together by candlelight, listening to soft foreign music by an artist I'd never heard of, eating the meal that he'd cooked for us and drinking red wine by the glassful. I hadn't known or thought about what to expect before arriving. He'd introduced me to his world, and that seemed an age ago now, although it was only two heavenly days earlier. Smoothing the table with his large hands in a circular motion, almost in preparation for his words, whilst still retaining the same cigarette between his fingers, reduced to almost a butt, he reached for his ashtray.

'Listen… I think we 'ave to be sensible about this,' he said.

'What do you mean?' I said, but already anticipating what he was about to say.

'The only way forward after this is a relationship, and I'm not sure it's a good idea for us to get involved like this,' he said. He was different towards me now, distant even. He looked down and played with the stub of his cigarette in the ashtray, rolling it around in his fingers. 'You're sensible, so in a way, it makes this a bit easier to say.' He drew a breath. 'You're living in England and I'm in Paris; 'ow's that going to work? We're never going to see each other. Distance relationships don't work; I've tried it before.'

Speechless and compounded by nerves at the brief shock of his words, it rendered me almost incapable of doing anything but go over what he'd said. Despite having denied it to myself, I knew he was making a choice… that damned letter. I'd desperately wanted to bury that knowledge, but it was apparent. Hearing the words spoken out loud, I wasn't reacting as coolly as I'd hoped. My thoughts were racing. Perhaps it wasn't just the letter; maybe it was me.

'I suppose you're right,' I said. The words came tripping out of my mouth without my brain engaging.

'I'm trying to do the right thing by both of us 'ere. It's only going to come to the point where we both end up getting 'urt, and that would be so much worse than just stopping it all now, before it starts.'

He didn't look at me. Didn't or couldn't, I wasn't sure. All I could do was stare.

He was still playing with the remains of the cigarette stub. Rolling it between his finger and thumb, making a pattern in the ash. It was probably helping him to concentrate, like doodling with a pen and paper on the phone and creating a small masterpiece by the time the conversation ends.

'It's selfish, I know,' he said.

'Well, if that's the way you really feel…' I trailed off. Perhaps I'd been too naïve. I hated myself and felt foolish and vulnerable for trusting him.

'No, it is selfish and I'm sorry. Sorry for 'aving got you over 'ere like this and then doing this to you. If I'd 'ave thought about it, I would 'ave told you not to come,' he said.

'Well, I'm glad I came… or I was until now. I tried not to let myself get too attached.'

I hadn't meant to say that part out loud. Feeling myself blush, I looked away, hating myself even more for revealing that I'd fallen for him all too fast. He glanced up at me.

'You don't get attached to someone in just a few days,' he said.

That just made it worse. And it wasn't true. It hadn't been just the last few days. Churning with emotion, I wasn't ready to give up. My eyes came to rest back on the sailing canvas, whilst biting my lip and trying to gather some words. A scene from *Titanic* played out in my head. After falling overboard, our hands were slipping away from each other, desperate to be rescued. Sinking my teeth too hard into my bottom lip, I blinked back my tears.

'I'm still coming to your party,' I said.

'Of course, you're welcome for the party. I didn't say it so you wouldn't come. You're always welcome 'ere. I'm not trying to cut ties with you – please don't think that. It's just that I don't think a relationship between us is possible, that's all, and it's not you if that's what you're thinking… I feel like I've known you for years,' he said.

'Do you?' I asked.

We caught each other's eyes. His words sparked a tiny glimmer of hope amidst the confusion.

'You make me feel like I'm fifteen again.' He laughed then thought for a while. 'It would be so easy to say… you're coming to my party in about three weeks and then when am I going to see you?' He shrugged. 'Who knows, if they close down the Paris base like it's rumoured… but I don't want to live in the UK.' He shrugged again. 'It might work.' We looked at each other. 'No, what am I saying? I know it would work.'

'Why won't you give me a chance?' I asked, barely able to speak.

He looked directly into my eyes.

'Because I think this is for the best,' he said.

'I just can't believe…'

'Yes, I realise it would be easy to…' he said, without finishing, even though I silently pleaded to hear the rest.

'Well, if I'm still coming to your party, I have between now and then to work on changing your mind,' I said, acting upbeat, although my thoughts were volatile. One rejection was bad enough. But I couldn't help myself.

'I suppose you do,' he replied.

The look of seriousness on his face warmed to a peep of a smile, and a hot pang of desire shot through my entire body, rightly or wrongly giving me just a slither of hope amidst all the upset. My brain went into hyperactive mode. Then feeling compelled not to accept the situation as final, adrenaline pumped around my body at a rate of knots, fuelled by an overwhelming need. I could sense my dignity fast draining away like sand slipping through an egg timer.

Back at university, I'd had the reputation of stalking the man I wanted until I got him. Nothing too extreme or weird, not like the 1980s film, *Fatal Attraction*, where a lady boils a bunny. It was winning the chase, although with Marc it was different.

'Well, I think I should warn you that I'm a very persistent and determined person. On those psychometric practice tests for interviews, the reports always say that about me,' I said. Then I cringed, feeling powerless to barricade my thoughts from converting into idiotic words.

'That's good for jobs,' he said.

'Not just jobs,' I replied.

He laughed. 'Sorry, I didn't quite mean that the way it sounded.'

'I have a sixth sense about these things, you know,' I said. And despite the need to stop, I continued to babble, splurging too much embarrassing and unnecessary stuff.

'Sixth sense – what is that?' he asked.

'It means I have intuition. Do you know what I mean?'

'Sure, I guess,' he said.

Catching sight of the picture again, I placed myself within the image of the large ship, balancing precariously on a pirate's plank, refusing to jump and not about to be shoved off. Maybe it was the haziness of the July summer sun, combined with the romance of being in Paris accompanied by an amazing Frenchman with serious potential. I simply couldn't allow him to toss everything overboard. Struggling to accept things, there was a current vacancy for the love of my life, and Marc had been a strong contender to fill that empty gap.

'And what is your intuition telling you now?' he asked.

'That you'll soon realise you made a huge mistake and wonder whether there's still a chance I may forgive you, and then you'll ask me to come back to Paris next weekend to do it all over again,' I said.

He laughed. Then his smile faded.

'But you're working, remember? You'll see I'm right about this. We would never see each other.'

'If it's worth having then it's never easy,' I said, almost begging him.

Distance didn't have to be a problem, although working schedules would be a battle, but not impossible. I'd convinced myself that it was worth a try. How could he so easily surrender to a bit of inconvenience and throw away what we'd started? That thought was never spoken out loud.

'Look, there is something that I 'aven't told you... I trust you not to say anything to anyone and I should 'ave told you before. I've only just 'eard.' He drew a breath, and I knew what he was about to say. 'I've been offered a job – it's a contract somewhere else. It's paying a lot of money, and I've accepted. It's going to take me to Indonesia, where I'll be based. I should 'ave told you. I'm sorry, but I didn't know 'ow things would turn out.'

I felt strangely relieved by his admission, not that I could reciprocate by mentioning my earlier discovery. But I'd had time to digest the initial shock of the job and its location. And I hadn't blindly ignored the plunging sensation it had triggered – just rationalised it. Surely, there was a way to be together if we tried. The logistics of us both working on an airline meant that being in a far-flung corner of the Earth didn't make it impossible.

'We both work on the airlines, we could still—' I began.

He cut in.

'Not only that – it's dangerous. I can't 'ave any connections, no links to anyone I've not already declared. I'm not even supposed to share that, so please, that's all I can tell you. I'm only going to be in Paris now for a matter of weeks,' he said.

His words sounded so unbelievable I almost laughed. Thank God I'd seen that bloody letter. Had I not seen it, I'd have concluded matters as an extreme attempt to avoid me.

Contemplating what had just been said, we both sat in silence for a moment, needing time to digest everything. Privately, I questioned whether I'd been a total mug, although I didn't entirely blame myself. There'd been plenty of encouragement on his part. Chemistry was a driving factor. Perhaps I'd just been too easily available and too easy a conquest. In the next instant, I tossed that thought aside as readily as it had invaded my thoughts. I was certain of his feelings for me. And I wanted him in my life, more than he knew.

'Think we both just got carried away,' he said, whilst slowly getting up from the table.

That wasn't true. Ever since the Paris night-stop where he'd passed me his details, he'd constantly been on my mind, like a flashing beacon, until I'd finally worked up the nerve to do something about it.

'Well, if not right now, then – later on maybe?' I said, trying to hide the desperation in my voice.

'In a couple of months, you'll meet somebody nice and I don't want you to miss out on that 'cos of me. You already said you don't like to turn down your opportunities. Go back to England and don't think about me. Forget *all* about me,' he said.

'What you're saying is impossible. I don't want to meet somebody else. I don't want to forget all about you, and *don't you dare* forget about me,' I said as I felt my throat tense and a sharp sting of tears well in my eyes.

'I won't,' he said. He took hold of my hand and lifted it to meet his mouth with a gentle kiss. 'Give me a mention in your book when you get around to writing it… a chapter… a page… a paragraph maybe? Wherever I am in the world, I'll buy it,' he said.

His smile faded to a look of sadness, most likely mirroring me after glancing at my face. I couldn't conceal my feelings, but I didn't want to cry. Biting on my sore lip kept further emotion from escaping.

'Think I can manage more than just a paragraph,' I said. Trying to be brave, but confusion rife in my head, a numbness prevailed. I took a step towards him. 'Give me a hug.' Reaching out, I wrapped my arms around him tightly, not wanting to let go. He held me, pulling me close for a second, before ever so gently taking my arms in his hands and withdrawing himself from my embrace. Almost resigned to his outcome and with a feeling of being able to say or do no more to change things, I let him go.

As I glanced at my watch, knowingly he picked up my bags. It was time to leave.

He opened the car door for me then got in, switching on the stereo. His favourite artist sang through the speakers again. Recognising it this time, I still didn't know the musician's name. We didn't share the same musical tastes.

We started the journey back to the airport. Passing by the tree-lined street reminded me of our earlier run together and how I'd been horrified when he way outpaced me, being a smoker. But he'd practised, and anyway, he wasn't so hot in his shorts. The sweaty image flashed in my mind. Glancing in his direction, I would get over him.

Then he smiled at me, reminding me of the feel of his lips and the thing he did with his tongue that injected a tingle with each kiss, and the sensation of his warm olive skin against mine. The whisper of his voice replayed in my head – *delicate English skin, so soft and smooth* – and how his fingers had wandered over me, stroking my exposed arms and torso and caressing my entire body. He knew how to do passion. No lover had come close to studying me in any detail the way he had. Life was cruel. He was going to take some getting over.

Allowing myself to watch him out of the corner of my eye, whilst he concentrated on the road, he looked properly French, wearing his navy lightweight jumper over his shoulders, indigo jeans and dark brown moccasin shoes. When he wasn't wearing his sunglasses, he had the most compelling dark eyes. More used to seeing him in uniform on the rare occasions when we had worked together – black trousers and white shirt – his uniform made him appear stockier than he was. His tousled dark hair somehow suited him that way, and the way he smoothed it over with his mannerism of running his fingers through it when he spoke to me. He looked tall, even when seated. It had amused me when I'd first seen him crouch down to almost climb into the cockpit through the small and narrow door. Similarly, at his home, which wasn't remotely typical of a Parisian apartment, the stairway was a bit too small for a man of his height. I'd been right about him having to bow his head to avoid the low lintel at the foot of his stairs.

The stereo filled a lack of conversation. I wondered more about his job. Obviously, he hadn't wanted me to ask more questions. And I couldn't blame him for placing a job above me; we hadn't known each other long. Well, not in the sense of being a proper couple – almost but not quite. One long date didn't count.

The air con still wasn't working properly. It was hot and sticky. I watched as he pulled off his jumper and flung it onto the back seat. I adjusted my window enough to enable a breeze. My hair went flying. I let it ruffle. It'd be frizzy by the time we arrived. I didn't care anymore.

We were already in the northern suburbs of Paris. I'd learned that you could never be sure about Parisian traffic. Coming to a busy intersection, he accelerated onto what looked like a motorway near the Stade de Paris and I let out a squeal.

'What is wrong?' he said, looking at me, his eyes wide.

'Sorry, I thought we were going to hit that car to the side of us,' I said.

He laughed. 'That's called positive driving. You must accelerate and go for it or else no one will let you in. That's a top tip for driving in Paris.'

Flushed with embarrassment, it was a useless *top tip* – I'd never need. Not now. We headed back to Charles de Gaulle Airport without further events.

♡

Arriving at departures, I went to pick up my suitcase from his car boot, but insistently he stopped me. He was adorable, opening doors for me and expecting to carry my bags. I was being dumped in the politest way possible. I'd been a sucker for a complete charmer. *Why did he have to be quite so perfect?* It made it all the harder. After checking on the flight information, we went outside in the sun. He lit up another cigarette.

'You asked me what my bad points were earlier today,' he began. 'Well, one of my good points, perhaps the best one, is that I'm very honest, and I hope you appreciate me being honest with you right now. It's better that I'm like this than going along with things and then never getting in touch with you again – don't you think?'

'Well, that would make you a bastard, and I would definitely change my mind about you then. But I know you're not. I actually think you're... quite lovely,' I said and regretted saying the last part, wishing I'd gagged myself and taped up my mouth.

'I think that about you too,' he replied softly, making me feel totally okay about having told him that he was *lovely*.

'You don't meet someone you have a connection with every day,' I said.

'Yes. I know... I know,' he replied.

He looked down at his feet. Standing against the terminal building, I watched him finish his cigarette as we sheltered from the hot sun.

'Won't do you any good,' I said. *God, I could be so fucking annoying at times – why did I say it?*

'You keep telling me that, but I'll do it anyway,' he replied, blowing out a wisp of smoke. I both loved and hated his stubbornness.

We stood together for the next couple of minutes in calm quietness. Thinking about our earlier conversation, I guessed he was doing the same. That's all that occupied my mind. Side by side, I clung to the last few minutes of being in his company, resigned to it being the final time.

'Think I'd better go and check in now, before they close the gate,' I said, acting a fake happy as I bent down to grab my bags.

'No, let me; it's the least I can do,' he said, reaching for my case. He carried it across to the gate and set it down.

'I suppose this is it then,' I said.

The pitch of my voice was giving way. I stopped talking and swallowed hard on the lump in my throat. My heart was pounding as he stood close.

'Please don't think of it as a casual hook-up – that's not what it was. Not what it was at all,' he said.

'I know,' I whispered.

'Please… think about what I've said to you. You'll go 'ome and realise that what I'm doing is right for both of us,' he said gently.

'You're so wrong. You keep in mind that I'm just a plane journey away.'

I stepped up to him and slowly kissed him. He kissed me back, then drew away. I kissed him tenderly a second time.

'Don't do that too much. Remember what we just talked about?' he said.

His lips trembled as he spoke. I stole a last kiss. He pulled away. His feet shuffled backwards. The expression in his eyes made me blink back the tears. But I couldn't contain them. I couldn't hide.

'I feel like such an asshole,' he said.

Fleetingly, our eyes met. He half raised his hand. I turned away.

THE FLIGHT HOME

The passenger lounge wasn't busy. Choosing a solitary row of seats, I waited to board the plane back home to England. I tried to think about anything other than Marc. But trying to exercise complete and sudden memory loss was impossible. Nothing was working. Any attempts at forgettery kept conjuring up inconvenient flashbacks.

Biting my lip, a few stray tears escaped. They were quickly banished with a swift flick of my hand. Determined to force a smile, I wasn't upset. That's what I told myself. My compact mirror said otherwise. As pools welled in my eyes, it reflected a crazy crying clown. I laughed, watching small streams spill from my eyes and trickle down my cheeks. Tricking myself was impossible. Surrounded by strangers, I watched as my dignity drained away in uncontrollable tears. Fumbling for tissues in my bag, I wiped away *panda eyes* from the runny splodges of black mascara that had smudged. Dabbing on some powder, it disguised my puffy blotchy appearance enough to avoid any awkward dilemmas with crew members.

A volcano of emotions continued to stir, but it was mainly contained, ready for an eruption at home. Emma would be the victim of that explosion. I needed her. She'd know what to do when everything poured out. She'd stop me drowning in melancholy and my own snot and tears. She'd glue me back together, loose pieces and all, like a fragmented bone china cup. Then she'd mop up the mess – all whilst trying to feed me chocolate biscuits, which I wouldn't fancy. I texted her:

Disaster. Coming home. Hope u r in when I'm back :(

Seconds ticked by. Nothing appeared back, just a black empty screen.

The plane wasn't full. Jim was on board. He stood at the back. When he saw me, he gave a familiar nod and a wink. Just seeing him almost moved me to tears again. The back row was empty. Being away from passengers enabled privacy to wallow in misery and self-pity.

I passed by a man ramming the remains of a burger in his face. I envied him, stuffing himself. Maybe he'd suffered multiple heartbreak and was comfort eating. *Is it possible to overcome hurt by squashing it with a stomach of junk food – preferably bucket-sized ice cream eaten with a shovel?* Even if it was, I couldn't face food.

'Hey, doll face. Could do with putting my feet up for a bit, I've worked my ass off today… Doll face, what's wrong with you?' said Jim.

'I'm okay. It's good to see you,' I said, trying to hide my face.

'You on your own?' he asked.

'Yeah.'

'You're not in uniform. Positioning? Just coming back from Paris?' he asked. I wriggled, starting to regret sitting at the back. Then Jim paused for a breath. 'Wait a minute.

Way hay hay, does this have something to do with *Marc* by any chance? But you're upset. What's gone on?'

I looked up. Jim had never been so sharp.

'It didn't work out okay. That's all you need to know. Don't tell anyone. I don't wanna be the latest gossip… or one of your stories,' I said.

'I wouldn't do that to you, doll face.' His face scowled, looking hurt.

'Sorry, I know.'

He pretended to zip his lips together and place an imaginary key into his jacket pocket.

'Do you need me to *duff 'im up for ya?* Like if he's been a bastard…' he asked.

'No,' I laughed. 'Things probably just weren't meant to be.'

'It's okay, chick,' he said. Then he put his arm around me, triggering more helpless tears. 'You won't want to hear this but whatever happened… he was mad keen. I'm telling you. Man, I was pleased to see you in France so I didn't have to listen to him. He bored the tits off me… blah blah blah and I told him. I mean you're great and everything, but he didn't half go on. I mean, who does that? So, whatever happened, if he's been a twat…' his voice trailed off.

'Why you tellin' me this now?' I said.

' 'Cos he didn't want me to say anything, and you know that's fuckin' hard for me, so I just gave you enough hints… See, I can be sort of discreet when it's necessary. Anyway, I better feed the freight. Shout if you wanna chat.'

'Thanks, Jim,' I said.

He tapped his nose and pointed his finger at me, then left. He'd never shown much, if any, sensitivity that I could previously recall.

He nipped back, holding up a small bottle of champagne.

'If you're not drinking now, then take it home for later,' he said and plonked it down on my tray table. I smiled, grateful of his attempt to apply a sticky plaster to my large, open wound.

When I arrived home, Emma was waiting.

'Come on then. Tell me everything,' she said in her *Mumsy* voice, which she didn't use often.

'You're back early,' I said, pleased to see her.

'Exercising flexitime. It wasn't busy, and I was due an afternoon off. Don't think anyone really noticed. So, what happened?' she asked.

I planted my face into her shoulder, only surfacing for air when it became uncomfortably damp and feeling my nose start to run.

'Sorry,' I blurted, between sobs.

'It's okay. Let it all out. Here – you might want to blow your nose,' she said, passing me a bunch of tissues. Then she hovered a plate in front of my face. 'Biscuit? It's chocolate.'

'You know I can't eat. I've just had my heart ripped out,' I blurted, between sobs.

'Hey, it was lust not love. And don't worry; I'm so starving I'll eat your share,' she said.

'You're a fat pig, but you're so good to me.'

'Good to see you still have a sense of humour. So... tell me everything,' she said.

By the time I'd finished recounting all the details of everything I could remember, she even knew the colour of his bedsheets.

'Do you think he actually liked me, or was he just out for a good time?' I asked.

'Don't be silly. He liked you. I think he just got it wrong. He had his reasons from what you've said. Sounds like things probably went better than expected, and he hadn't really thought it through, you know, with the job and everything.'

'He said he was being honest. Told me it was his best quality. Only got his word for it, though,' I said.

'True, but why would anyone go to so much effort? I think the timing was out... the job and you in the UK. It'd make it pretty hard. A case of bad timing,' she said.

'Will you stop taking his side? I would have pulled out all the stops,' I said.

'I know,' she laughed, chomping on another biscuit. 'You're always Mrs Persistent about the things you want. But listen, get under someone to get over someone. You'll meet somebody else.'

'No way, I'm done with the whole love thing,' I said.

'I already told you it was lust, not love,' she said.

'Yeah, lust,' I repeated.

'Maybe we should get away together for a bit. Like a mini-break. Have some fun. You can use your airline perks on me,' she said, sort of half-joking whilst yawning. She looked at her watch. 'It's late and I'm on duty tomorrow, and those books won't hit the shelves without me.'

'Thanks, mate. Sorry I've gone on about it all night. And maybe you're right about going away and having some fun together,' I said.

'You'd do the same for me. We'll put off talking party plans until you're ready,' she said.

'What d'yu mean? I'm not going to any party. Did any of what I've just said sink in?' I asked.

'You say that now... but I know you,' she smirked. 'Sleep on it. We'll discuss it later, okay?'

'I've just been dumped, well sort of. What idiot would put themselves through that sort of torture? Whatever it was, he doesn't want to see me again,' I said.

'Talk later. Put it on hold for now. G'night,' she said and slunk off to bed.

I turned on the TV. There was no point in me going to bed.

FRENCH KISSING RULES

A few days later

It was Saturday morning and I had yoga class, without Emma. Our usual teacher had been away on a retreat. Emma hadn't liked the temporary instructor so had skipped the classes in favour of skating. Apparently, she was becoming a disco diva on wheels.

Grateful for some alone time, I arrived early at the village hall. The door was unlocked. Jessie breezed through with her usual bright smile. Surprised to see her, I'd tell Emma later. She'd be disappointed to miss out on Jessie's class, despite skating.

Jessie wore her usual patchwork baggy trousers, the sort I'd never get away with, without looking ridiculous. Her cheerful trousers suited her personality. And she could say things I couldn't, like *When you do things from your soul, it's like a river running through your body.* The aura of her happy persona rubbed off, always making me feel great. I wondered if she continually felt how I did after each of her sessions.

We always began with a short period of quiet breathing on our mats, to relax our mind. Sometimes thoughts of work would creep in at the start. And it was one of those days. It required a deeper mode of relaxation by focussing on breathing, to let go of everything.

Starting with our yoga positions or *asanas*, as I'd learned, we did the limbering warm-up moves. Jessie was telling us something about our minds being like a chariot attached to powerful horses, each with different names, like one was *Breath* and another was *Desire*. Apparently, the chariot pulled in the direction of the more powerful animal. Images of Marc flashed up, making it hard to focus on a yoga mood, and even harder when Jessie continued to bang on about the horse named *Desire*.

'Breathe. If you allow it to take control then your mind is agitated and troubled,' said Jessie in a calm, soothing voice.

Helplessly, I pictured Marc on a horse dressed as a gladiator. The harder I tried to push the image away, the more it stayed fixed. *Focus*, I pleaded and *breathe*. Uncontrollable fantasies were a problem.

Jessie went around the room giving each of us *a little love*, as she called it, by placing her hands on our chest during corpse pose or *Savasana*. It was supposed to help our bodies relax into the earth and to release a little tension, rejuvenating our bodies and minds. But fantasies continued to mess with my mind as I pictured Marc riding away on a horse with me in his chariot.

Then I felt Jessie's hands on my feet as she massaged them. The gentle kneading of my feet felt good. It wasn't something she usually did, but I felt tense. *Who knew what new tricks she'd learned on her retreat – could yoga teachers sense pure lust and a yearning libido?* I blushed. Jessie moved on.

Emma and I had arranged to meet in the Penthouse later that Saturday afternoon. On arriving home, I found Emma in the bathroom, testing out a new bottle of red hair dye. The discarded box of evidence, *fiery fusion* lay visible on the sofa next to a stack of post. I thumbed through.

'Won't be long,' she shouted.

'Shit, I got an interview. That long-haul job I applied for.'

'That's great. Thought you didn't think you'd get it,' she said.

'I didn't, but looks like I've got a chance,' I said.

'Well, maybe we should go out for lunch, treat ourselves. Celebrate you getting an interview. And there's no food in,' she said.

'Let's do that,' I replied.

'Cool.'

'Jessie was back. She asked about you. Told her you'd got into skating, but you'd be back,' I said.

'Gutted,' she replied. 'I'm going next week.'

'Not if we've booked that mini-break, you're not,' I said.

'Forgot about that. Week after then,' she replied.

'Deal.'

Pushing aside the cardboard packaging and paper instructions, I sat down with a magazine I'd bought from the newsagent on the way home. With a mention of something French on the cover, I'd bought it spontaneously and thumbed through for the article, *French Kissing – romantic encounters with Frenchmen*. There was a column detailing various European men, but it was just the French that interested me. Finding the page and predicting that it couldn't tell me anything I didn't already know, I read it. Then huffed.

'Ems, listen to this. Can you hear me?' I shouted.

'Yep. What?' she shouted back.

'A first kiss with a Frenchman is akin to the beginning of a romantic relationship.'

'You on about him *again*?' she said.

'Listen. Apparently, that initial kiss means that you are now, officially, his girlfriend – well, according to this article. It also says that *if a Frenchman kisses you, he means business.* And get this last bit – *don't go kissing any Frenchmen if you're not in it for the long haul.*' I threw down the magazine, crossing my arms. 'What *fuckwittery!*'

'Ha ha. Feeling short-changed? Well, that's a lesson in *don't believe everything you read,* and maybe you just kissed a defective one. There's bound to be a few of those around,' she said.

Emma appeared from the bathroom with a towel over her shoulders. Her hair was compacted in a mass, piled on top. And drips of red hair dye were streaked across the top of her forehead.

'It's no good blaming the magazine,' she said.

'Well, according to what it says in there, it's his way of sealing the deal and making sure you're exclusively his. Then you can expect dramatic declarations of love to soon follow, and it's all part of the package of dating a Frenchman, being swept along with the romance of the culture. What *bollocks!* Do you think I should maybe send him a copy, so he knows what he was supposed to do?'

'Do you think you might be getting a bit carried away? Look, maybe try another one, better luck next time. Or is it third time lucky? Kiss enough frogs and you'll find a prince,' she laughed. 'Anyway, you did more than that.'

'Well, I wouldn't do it again,' I said.

'Bullshit. And you know it. If he showed up here, you'd be chewing his face off and ripping his clothes off for bedroom athletics before the poor guy even had a chance.'

'Well, I'd like a chance… he knew how to deliver the perfect champagne kiss and I wanted that Frenchman, defective or not,' I said.

'Champagne kiss!' she looked at me, deluded. 'Just find another. There's a whole nation of them out there to work your way through. Or pick a different country and try another flavour. You've always been so vanilla in your taste,' she said.

'Cheeky cow.' I scowled back. She blew me a kiss and disappeared into the bathroom.

'But you love me really. Won't be long, I'm starving. And you can tell me all about the plans. I'm *sooo* excited about Spain,' she said.

Sun and Sangria

The benefits of working for an airline included heavily discounted staff travel and available last-minute mini-breaks to Spain.

Money wasn't such a restriction, unlike in the past. And the flights were so cheap, I booked two tickets to Seville and a hotel by the coast.

'Come on, Emma; I'll hold your hand,' I said, trying to coax her towards the boarding gate.

'It's all right for you. I suppose you think I'm being ridiculous getting scared of flying. You probably think of it like walking down the street and then finding you need to cross the road but getting scared in case you get knocked down by a car,' she said.

'No. I've never thought of flying like that. You'll be fine, but we need to board NOW,' I said.

'Will you stop tugging on my arm?' she moaned.

'Yes, once you board the plane. I know you don't like flying, but I didn't know you had an actual pain-in-the-ass full-on phobia about it,' I said.

'It's not a phobia. It's just a rational fear of not liking aeroplanes. It's okay for you. I don't do this every day,' she said.

'You're gonna be okay. Take a breath. Ready?' Emma nodded and took hold of my hand. 'Let's go,' I said.

We joined the back of the queue at the boarding gate.

'Should be all right. I'm wearing my lucky pants today,' she muttered under her breath.

'Excellent. You're all set for tonight then. Plus, you'll be all right with a spot of turbulence.' Gauging the reaction on her face, it had been the wrong thing to say.

'I'm not the dirty whore,' she said.

'Bitch,' I said. 'But I'll forgive you, only 'cos you're nervous of flying.' Emma was a wreck. I only hoped it wouldn't be a turbulent flight.

Turbulence made things interesting, especially on a working flight. When the captain switched on the seatbelt signs, which was inevitable in turbulence, it enabled a quick yet bumpy dash down the aisle with a trolley. The bonus being void of any toilet interruptions, enabling fast retirement onto a crew seat with a piece of cherry cake and a miniature can of something fizzy – provisions permitting. I'd become proficient in the art of balancing in the aisle with a trolley for support whilst pouring a drink, complete with a smile of course. It was a circus act. It reminded me of skiing. Riding out the unexpected bumpy bits or moguls as I later learned, all whilst remaining intact on two feet. I'd learned that planes were built to withstand thunderstorms. But secretly I wondered how well they'd stand up to a bad storm.

'Just a minute,' she said, 'let's go and have a look out of the window.'

'Why?' I asked.

She grabbed my arm.

'Which plane do you think we'll be on? I just want to make sure it looks okay before I get on,' she said. I groaned. Giving in, we walked over to the window. I pointed out the little fifty-seater plane parked up on stand. 'As small as that? Well, I suppose it's less likely to fall out of the sky with less weight,' she said.

'Completely. That's exactly how it works,' I said, unable to resist teasing. She scowled. 'Look at that,' she pointed, 'let's watch the big one.'

From the window of the departures lounge, we could see a large jet on the approach, coming in to land. As it got closer, my thoughts turned to a daydream about Marc being the pilot. The sun glistened off its bodywork. It touched down and glided along the landing strip, like a model on a catwalk. Slowing its pace, it performed a turn, taking up centre stage. Then it faced the passenger terminal in all its glory, before parking on stand in full view of admirers. Ceremoniously and proudly displaying its full wingspan, like an eagle, it was ruler of the airfield, proud and powerful, morphing the smaller planes into insignificance.

'Right, you can start doing your caring hostess bit by looking after your nervous flyer,' she said, snapping me back to reality. I sighed.

'Caring? You got the wrong industry for that. They'd probably be slagging you off in the galley and then putting on their best two-faced act when they spoke to you,' I said.

'Really?' she asked.

'Depends on the crew,' I added.

'Best pretend not to be scared then,' she said.

'Exactly. Spain, here we come.'

We flopped into our seats.

'Busy, isn't it?' she said.

'Want a magazine?' I asked.

I offered her a copy of *Glamour*, hoping to distract her. She took the bait. The cabin was rammed like cattle being herded. It was the usual hubbub of commotion until passengers eventually found their seats. Then I noticed a woman in a panic. She was examining the air filters with the smoke coming through the vents. I knew instantly what was going through her mind. There was a standard passenger announcement for the cabin pressure equalising and causing a temporary bout of air through the vents, which appeared smoke-like. The cabin crew just hadn't managed to make the announcement yet; they were too busy ferrying the herds. The aircraft wasn't on fire. I sat and observed as she started flapping her arms about for the attention of cabin crew. I was about to nudge Emma, then thought better of it. I had enough of a job providing reassurance to my priority nervous flyer.

The flight time to Spain took ages. I was pleased. It would have disappeared in five minutes, had I been working it. There was usually so much to do before reaching the destination – teas and coffees, snacks, gashing in, setting up for the next flight and remembering to remove one's plonky kit from the stowage cupboard. The plonky kit was an interesting name for what was basically a small case that contained ice tongues, a bottle opener, a calculator, plus anything else useful that could be stuffed in there. I'd replaced my plonky kit twice already, because of having left it in the ice tray, which then got removed with the trollies. Mysteriously, they vanished into aeroplane world never to be seen again, just like the lost property office that collected all manner of items that never seemed to be reunited with their owners, except plonky kits didn't make it there; I checked. And ice tongues only ever seemed to exist in the big supermarkets, which was a real *bugger* because it meant finding time to make a trip out to somewhere you'd rather not be just to replace items you'd no doubt leave on board again… at some point.

Fascinated with the views from the window, this time I could indulge myself, watching everything, undisturbed by passengers. The rays of sunshine were so intense, I put on my sunglasses. Dreamily, I peered at the puffy clouds. They looked like layered cake in streaks of marmalade orange and pink grapefruit hues. The pretty pastel shades of fluffy, textured candyfloss looked like it would taste good if only I could get close enough to stick out my tongue to lick the sweetness. My stomach rumbled. I was hungry.

When the clouds parted over Spain, they revealed rivers streaking across the land, with smaller, more delicate ripples escaping like marbles and forming pretty patterns. It looked Spanish even from way up high. Dark golden patches were visible, reminding me of my eyeshadow palette with its sultry tones and the sparkle of glitter in my bronzing kit. It was a contrast to the lush greens of England we'd left behind, which reminded me of lawnmowers.

Tiny formations of black dots were visible in neat rows. I had no idea what they were, but in my mind's eye they'd become intricate rows of olive trees, ready for the olive pickers, whose crop ended up on the shelves of shops and then occasionally my olive bowls on a Friday night with Emma.

'Olive?' said Emma, almost telepathically.

She passed me a box of mixed nuts and offerings she'd brought with her on the plane. They matched the image on the box in just the same way I imagined them growing on trees – all fat, ripe and juicy. If she'd have bought them on the plane, they would have been drained of life. Starving, I wasted no time in wolfing them down.

Emma had relaxed her dieting rule for our holiday. I was glad. She was less cranky and more fun when she wasn't denying herself pleasures. She'd already put away a hefty bacon sandwich with lashings of tomato sauce whilst en route to departures.

'We're almost coming in to land,' I said, feeling the plane slowly descend just as the seatbelt sign illuminated. Emma needed mental preparation for landing.

'Get out those boiled sweets you bought,' I said, reminding her. She rifled through her bag and popped one into her mouth. 'Good. Now suck on it like you're giving a blow job.' She coughed and spluttered and almost choked, as we laughed. 'Honestly, it'll help your ears on the descent. Promise.'

I reached inside her bag and took one for myself. We both faced each other, sucking on sweets with exaggerated determination. As the plane descended, we both concentrated hard on achieving a satisfying pop-in-the-ears sensation.

'You've serviced some lucky fellas,' I said, as we landed with a jolt. Emma's eyes widened. 'Don't worry, there's not a pilot alive who hasn't bumped a plane down the runway,' I reassured her, just as the passengers started to clap and give a cheer. 'I read somewhere that ninety-five per cent of flying is boredom and the other five percent is sheer terror,' I continued, as Emma looked at me in horror. 'Only joking,' I smiled, crossing my fingers.

After going through the rigmarole of passport control and collecting our bags, we made our way towards the car hire desk, stopping off briefly at an airport shop to stock up on supplies for the journey. We negotiated paying and bundled some sandwiches, fruit and plenty of junk food into our bags.

The Spanish seaside hadn't looked far away on a map. I figured we'd head to Cadiz and then consult a more detailed map to find the exact location of Chiclana de la Frontera, where we'd booked a good hotel, again on mates' rates courtesy of Jet Xpress. I prayed that Emma's map reading would suffice, seeing as I was the driver and wasn't sure that my skills, or lack of, would get us there. We headed to the loos. I couldn't chance having to deviate off route to find a service station.

The car hire was a brave decision. Not only was driving on the wrong side of the road, meaning *the right*, quite unnatural to me, but hiring an unfamiliar car took me out of my comfort zone. We should have booked a transfer, but it was too late now.

'How far away is it?' I asked the Spanish rep at the desk.

'About two hours' driving,' she said.

I turned to Emma, pulling a face.

'*Shit*. A foreign car, abroad and driving on the wrong side,' I said.

'You'll be fine,' she said.

What if I crash the car? What if we get really lost? What if we end up breaking down and no one speaks English? A whole load of imaginable nightmare scenarios played out in my mind as panic beguiled me.

'Todos est bueno,' said the rep, smiling. Then she handed me the car keys.

'What's that mean?' asked Emma.

'It means everything's fine. I bet she says that to everyone.'

I grasped the keys.

After a couple of *faux pas* reversing manoeuvres, I got the hang of the gear stick. My toe tickled the pedal to make it move, but anything was more powerful than my little Mini.

'Who needs a massive horse power, whatever that means, when driving in a foreign country on the wrong side of the road, unless you're a racing driver?' I said.

'Why'd you book it then?' asked Emma.

'It's what came up,' I replied.

With a firm white-knuckle grip of the steering wheel, we set off, feeling a bit *Thelma and Louise,* movie style. Except we were polar opposites, having had a *wee* and with sandwiches at the ready we'd prepared. Possibly, I was turning into my mother.

Taking it slow, I thought about annoying Sunday drivers holding up traffic. And driving like a snail. Just like me. I wouldn't be so impatient with Sunday drivers in future.

♡

Approximately two long hours later and having successfully negotiated obstacles such as roundabouts, toll booths en route and distracting statues of black bulls on hillsides, we pulled up at *Hotel del Sol*.

'Well, that was a bloody miracle. How did we manage that?' I said, turning off the engine.

'Yeah. Was a bit worried when you handed me the map, but I didn't wanna say,' replied Emma.

We got out, stretched and soaked up the heat of the intense sun.

'Yoga on the beach here will be fab,' I said, pulling the suitcases from the car boot.

'I'm parched. I might have to drink the sea if we don't find some water,' said Emma.

At reception, we were each handed a welcome glass of cava. We knocked it back, despite a deep thirst.

'Not too shabby here,' said Emma. The place looked decent, not five-star fancy, but smart enough with its polished mosaic floor tiles. Emma helped herself to a second full glass from the tray and sank it as fast as the first, whilst I read a leaflet about the black bulls we'd spotted on the hillside. They were associated with the sherry of the region. But the more interesting part mentioned a correlation between the number of bulls spotted tying in with the amount of conquests that were guaranteed for the evening. It was a challenge I wouldn't put to the test.

We found our room, dumped our bags, drank the free bottled water and wasted no time getting changed into bikinis.

'My God, look at the size of my paunch,' I complained to Emma, whilst gawping at the mirrored reflection from all angles.

'Yeah. Two babies in there at least,' she said, patting my rounded belly.

'You've got a bloat-on too.' I prodded her tummy.

'Yeah, it'll be fine once I've had a massive poo. It's just junk food swimming around,' she said matter-of-factly.

'Gross.' She adjusted her bikini briefs, pulling them lower. 'What you doing?' I asked.

'Making them look smaller,' she said. 'The larger you are on top, the smaller you want your bottom half to balance out body shape. I read that in the magazine you gave me on the plane.'

'Just showing off, you mean,' I said. Emma had ample boobage. 'Anyway, who cares? Let's go.'

I grabbed the beach bag, sun cream and sunglasses and almost forgot the room card on our way out.

'Wait,' said Emma, pulling me back in. She picked up the remains of leftover fruit from the journey and threw them into my bag. 'We might get hungry.' I didn't argue, despite the shoulder strap digging into my flesh with the added weight. 'Wait one more minute.'

'What now?' I asked, getting impatient. She put her hand to her ear.

'I can hear the beach calling for two sexy beach babes,' she said.

'Clearly it's not calling for us then,' I said, closing the door.

Stepping outside into the heat, there was a fresh breeze on our side of the hotel. In the shade, it engulfed my body, causing a brief shivery sensation of goosebumps. Then the sun kissed away the temporary chilliness, making me smile.

The vast expanse of deep blue ocean stretched out before us. It filled me with a calm serenity, like a yoga vibe. Occasional gusts of wind picked up particles of sand to scatter like salt.

'This spot right here will do nicely,' said Emma, spreading her towel over the sand.

I sat down and sprawled out next to her. I loved the beach. It smelled of summer holidays – salty sea air mixed with coconut sun cream. As I removed my plimsolls, the warm sand scrunched between my toes.

The ocean roared, and waves crashed, partially drowning out the distant and muffled cries of children playing. As I relaxed back, a sudden gust blew a dusting of sand over both of us. It clung to my body as I tried to brush it off. And it rubbed my skin like fine grade sandpaper.

'It's like showering with body scrub,' said Emma.

Shaking off my towel like a dusty old rug, I nestled back down to bask in the sunshine. Emma had been chuntering away but I'd barely paid attention. The cava was setting in nicely.

'Have you listened to anything I've been saying, or are you still driving yourself mad over this guy?' she said.

'Not everything. But I was doing okay until you just bought him up,' I said.

I hadn't mentioned Marc since the airport. The idea was to forget all about him, just like he'd told me to. And I had an interview to try and focus on now.

'I know what's going on; you're too quiet,' she said, fiddling with her bikini top. 'Think of it like this – you'll never end up like a couple of dried-up old peaches. A tired version of two old people who've run out of things to say to each other because they've said everything there is to say. Think of it as having been more an exotic and juicy pineapple type experience,' she said, pushing up both boobs with a satisfactory glance.

'Or a couple of ripe melons,' I joked, lifting my tits to imitate Emma.

'Plunge,' we both said in unison as we turned to each other and laughed at our exaggerated cleavages. It was our favourite word when discussing boobs. It first began as teenagers when Emma discovered the effects of plunge bras and it still amused us.

'I'm just trying to show you that you probably got all the best exciting bits before things turned sour and drooped, which everyone knows always happens, especially if he's older,' Emma said. She reached inside the bag and pulled out a banana, then pretended to let it flop, in her hand. 'Wilting willy syndrome.'

'He's not that old,' I giggled. 'Anyway, let's forget it.'

I used my beach bag like a pillow, propped my head up against it and watched the boats on the horizon. Spotting three, I wondered if Marc had sailed here. Then I berated myself for thinking about him. It was Emma's fault. She'd turned on a light bulb in my head.

'Any totty on the beach today?' she said, casually gazing around. 'Ooh, check out two o'clock.'

Unexpectedly, I took in an eyeful of crotch displayed by a fat old man having fallen asleep in his deckchair. He was tanned, leathery and wearing a small pair of dark briefs.

'Eww. You're so wicked,' I laughed. 'Don't think I need any more *totty* for now. Not like that anyway.'

'You know what they say?' she said.

'Yep. You told me. Get under someone to get over someone. Top advice, but I'm more selective than that, so I'll pass for now,' I said.

Inhaling the air, I tried to relax. Thankfully, Emma went quiet. Peacefully, I listened to the sea and observed the different bodies unashamedly exposed with kit off, getting their skin kissed by the sun.

An old man with a large stomach trotted by. The flab hung over his shorts with a lot of wobble and sagging. *Do old women find old men attractive when they reach the same age?* The concept of ageing without worry was appealing. Maybe I'd live happily by the sea in old age and let it all sag. That's where Marc was going to live. *Why can't I get him off my mind?*

The man became hidden behind a couple. Their skin was pale white, almost blue; they had to be either English or German. The man was wearing long brown socks on the sand and carrying his leather sandals – my money was on him being British. Next was a pretty slim girl with hooped earrings and her hair piled high. *Was she Marc's type?* Silently, I cursed Emma. I'd kept him at bay until the banana stunt.

'There's so many women with their baps out,' Emma said. It was true. The displays of plentiful breasts reminded me that I wasn't in the UK.

'It's not for me. They've got a kit-off sauna in the spa too. I'm no prude but I'm no way up for that,' I said.

'Me neither. Not till I've been on a diet. Anyway, you've got good baps,' said Emma.

'You been looking?' I asked.

'Couldn't help noticing your hooters earlier,' she said, 'they were virtually in my face when you were tucking them into your bikini.'

'Well, they're not like your knockers – they are the BIGGEST handful,' I said, pretending to weigh them.

'Well, these babies are going to waste right now,' she said, peering down at herself.

'That makes two of us then. I'd be up for a decent pair of hands to do the same.' I sighed.

'And we both know whose hands,' she teased.

'You're not doing a good job of getting me to move on,' I said.

'Soz. Maybe let's grab an ice cream. It's *scorchio*.'

We left our stuff. There was nothing worth nicking. The sand burned the soles of my feet, making me wish I'd worn flip-flops too, like Emma. Close to the sea edge, we stopped. I stood on the damp sand and felt relief from the heat. I watched the toing-and-froing ebb of the tide and the ripples gather momentum until they travelled further up and spilled over my feet. Their coldness was a pleasant shock.

We paddled. The water felt freezing. But we ventured further in as the waves flooded over my feet and legs and a second pelt took the water just above my knees unexpectedly. The cold caused me to draw a sharp intake of breath and giggle.

Heading over to the small beach shack café, I noticed how imprints of seagulls' feet were left behind like tridents stamped in the sand. It was a sign and I was being tormented by the devil.

'Oh, go away,' I said out loud.

'Why? You not getting fed up of me already, are you?' Emma asked.

'Just talking to the madman living in my head,' I replied.

'That's okay then.'

We passed a guy with a wild carpet of black chest hair. I'd never seen such a thick and bushy growth on a man's chest. Judging by the extended stare that Emma gave him, neither had she.

'Can you imagine him getting a wax?' I asked, whilst cringing at the thought of the used wax paper.

'Don't. That's foul,' said Emma, sticking two fingers in her mouth, pretending to gag and vomit. 'I'm wiping that thought. You'll put me off ice cream.'

We successfully negotiated buying ice cream via the well-known language of international pointy method. Each of us settled on a Cornetto of dark chocolate. It was less trouble choosing the same and to mutter the word *dos* rather than ask for two different flavours. Then we went full Spanish and ordered a couple of sangrias via the same method.

Getting back to our spot, the air was soon filled with a waft of cigarette smoke. Out of curiosity, I turned onto my tummy to lazily peruse the offender – a man with moobs, a huge belly, moustache and a tan. He was lying next to a big bottom clad in white briefs, also tanned. He spoke or sort of grunted at her in a deep, husky voice. She was probably his wife. I imagined them being a functional couple, long past the stage of romantic passion, but being a comfort to each other. I had no idea what he was saying, but as I licked my ice cream, I pictured him riding a bull, rodeo style. His voice seemed to fit the image, although maybe in his younger days. My inquisitive thoughts turned to the couple along with the associated knowledge of the black bull statues from earlier. They were going at it rodeo style. The repugnant image replayed without a stop button. My ice cream became less appetising.

Urgently, I rolled onto my back and tried to refocus. My line of sight caught a young, dark-haired, bronzed and well-defined man in skimpy briefs – the type requiring the right package. That was more like it. He reminded me of Marc, in a foreign way. Naked in my mind's eye, he swung freely and knocked against his own thighs. Then he strutted into the sea and tackled the waves with ease as the sea caressed his muscles before he dived in. A prize bull. And on top in a filthy dirty rodeo conquest.

'You okay?' Emma asked.

'Yeah, course. Why?' I asked.

'You're too quiet. This guy has really got into your head,' she said. Emma was right. Like a horribly horny teenage boy with raging hormones, I was constantly thinking about sex. I couldn't share my perverted thoughts. She'd confirm it was weird.

We both picked up our drinks. Emma sucked up the remainder of her sangria through the black straw then stirred the fruit left at the bottom, before thoughtfully picking it out and popping it into her mouth a bit at a time.

'Well, how about you don't forget all about him? It's obvious you don't want to,' she said.

'What you on about? The whole point of coming here was to wipe my memory,' I said.

'Don't bite my head off, but what if you go to his party? Wouldn't it at least be a bit of fun?' she said.

'I can't do that,' I winced.

'Why not?' she said

'Let me think about that… oh yes, I remember; because he won't want me there,' I said.

'You told me he said you were welcome. What you got to lose?' she asked, looking at me with her serious face.

'He said that before we met up. And people say all sorts of things they don't mean,' I said.

'He won't mind. It's only a party he invited you to. Anyway, I'll come and hold your hand. I wanna see this Romeo for myself. Find out if he's worth it. Then when I discover he's not, I can kick your arse back into reality. Oh yes… and I quite fancy continuing to be an international jet-setter with you. I could get used to this lifestyle. Spain one week, Paris the next. Anyway, when is it?'

'Sunday 24th,' I replied.

'Sunday? Who has a party on a Sunday?' she asked.

'People working on aeroplanes, aircrew – that's who. Anyway, you'd have to book off the Monday,' I said.

'No problemo. If you're up for it, then so am I,' she said, raising two thumbs up.

Emma was right about him playing on my mind. A whirlpool of thoughts still spun in my head, despite having promised her I'd forget all about him. She knew I wasn't capable.

The sangria had turned warm. I jabbed at the remains with my straw, mainly fruity chunks of apple left floating at the bottom. Standing the beaker in the sand, I left the rest.

'Fuckit. Okay. You're on,' I said.

'That's more like it. Hurray.' She clapped. 'We'll sort the details later. For now, let's get back to sunbathing and totty-spotting. Oh, and you're not allowed to change your mind. We're going, it's final,' she added.

The warm sun soaked through my body, making me feel good. I allowed myself to fantasise freely. I smiled. A little rainbow of contentment flourished in me, knowing I would see him again.

A Girls' Night In

It was fizzy wine Friday night and I'd been willing it to arrive. Having battled the airline assessment centre the day before, I was determined to enjoy myself. And despite having to work the Saturday, I wasn't due in early. We'd topped up our glasses with the remnants of pink fizz, and had decided to play 007 smoking gun cocktails, partly due to having run out of sparkling wine and partly due to the lyrics that boomed from the stereo. My eighties double CD set was on. The Human League was playing *Don't You Want Me*, sparking the idea for our cocktail game, all whilst chair dancing to the beat and simultaneously scoffing mouthfuls of crisps.

Emma's latest charity shop investment was being put to good use. Her complete set – well, almost – of retro champagne glasses, minus the one that was missing, adequately assisted our game. Their bowl shape reminded me of my gran's delicate glasses that she displayed on the top shelf of her kitchen unit. They made brief appearances on special occasions before immediately being washed, dried, then put back in place. Holding the stem of the glass, it felt familiar. And with each sip, thoughts of my gran's kitchen gradually blotted away.

186

The topic of conversation was Marc, again, or it had been before we'd turned up the volume. There'd been enough time between having a holiday and getting back to change my mind about Marc's party about a *zillion* times. There were so many reasons why it wasn't a good idea. Amidst the *zillions*, we'd already booked the tickets to Paris on a whim. But I hadn't fully committed to whether I had the balls to attend his party. My mind was busy, tossing around the idea.

'His invite probably doesn't still apply. We've not been in touch,' I said.

'It won't matter. Let's go anyway,' Emma said, as she knocked back the last of the cheap pink fizz, but we liked to pretend it was *champers*. Her eye was resting on a bottle of lager, which she'd easily down, prior to cocktail making.

'But what if he tells me to get lost or something? Oh my God, can you imagine what that would be like? Or maybe he's got a girlfriend. That would make sense about him not being able to see me again,' I said.

'We've been over that. Just chill. He doesn't sound like the type. But maybe you should let him know we're coming,' she said.

'Yeah. No! Hang on a minute. What if he tells us not to come? We'd end up not being able to go. Maybe I'll send him an email… a couple of days before. That way he won't get the chance to tell us not to,' I said.

'Might ring you on your mobile,' Emma said.

'I won't answer,' I said.

'Devious. I like it. So, are we going?' she asked, looking at me for an answer. 'Are we going or what?' she demanded.

'*Fuckit*. What the hell. Okay!' I said.

'Yay,' she shouted, high fiving me with her spare hand, whilst lifting the bottle of lager to her lips with the other. We toasted our agreement. As her bottle chinked my glass, I was reminded how wine always had that sort of relaxing *don't give a shit* kind of effect. 'You just needed a bit more encouragement and a whole lot of alcohol. Luckily, I'm here to get your ass to that party. Just call me your fairy godmother,' she said.

'Well, call me Cinderella,' I said.

'Wicked! I can't wait.' Emma giggled. 'I like this devious streak. Must be living with me that's doing you a favour.'

She was exactly the right person to talk me into doing something stupid with her misbehaviour and devilish sense of adventure. She was exactly who I needed on my arm at the party.

In a wave of excitement, we got off our chairs, throwing ourselves around the room. We danced to the remainder of *Don't You Want Me* before crashing back down again.

There wasn't much for us to lose. *We,* in partnership, didn't have anything to lose. There was more at stake for me, such as damage to my pride, dignity and self-respect. But if we flew to Paris knowing a party was happening and avoided it because of the potential to make fools of ourselves or acting like *a couple of tits,* as Emma often described our antics, then it would be wasting an opportunity for a whole lot of fun. And the chance to attend another Parisian party was never likely to present itself again.

'This calls for cocktail celebrations,' Emma said, reaching for the gun.

She'd bought the dodgy cocktail firing gun from the market after seeing a guy in full-swing hard-sell sales pitch, pretending to be James Bond. She'd been his victim. To her delight, she'd discovered that it fired out cocktail recipes. There were only five recipes, one for each chamber, but that was adequate for us. Taking it in turns, each of us became the female version of James Bond, firing off bullets in random directions. The other player had to run after the bullet. The timer allowed one minute to make the cocktail, including locating the bullet, which ended up in all manner of our kitchen orifices. (There was this time when it got wedged above the cupboard door and ceiling, and I'd tried to lift Emma in a fit of laughter and tears; then I'd nearly wet myself as she fell over, screaming, still clinging to the broom handle to poke it out.) The player had to make the cocktail recipe before the timer caused a *bang-bang*. Cocktail complete – within set time – then James Bond downed it. Whomever finished making the most cocktails after firing five rounds was the winner, although we usually lost track.

Setting out the ingredients, mainly vodka, rum, sugar, dried-up mint leaves and a bit of Blue Curacao, we got started. Mojitos were my favourite. Emma's coordination was always a bit lacking. She usually ran around like a donkey, trying to grab the bullet.

After playing two games, which involved ten cocktails (they were only minis), I blew the tip of the gun, declaring myself the winner. Emma pretended to act sozzled, rolled her eyes and stuck out her tongue.

'I'm so 'cited to be goin' to a party in Paris,' she slurred.

'Me too!' I laughed.

It was settled. We would gatecrash his party, sort of. I didn't know if the invite still stood, which made it seem like a game of truth or dare, half-crazy but fun. Excitement pelted through my body.

'What you wearin' then?' she asked.

'No idea. You?' I said.

'Something seductive… quite fancy meeting a Frenchman, but he must be rich of course,' she said.

She meant every word. If we were gatecrashing, we owed it to ourselves to do it in style. It would cost a small fortune, but it would be worth it. I was now pleased she'd blown me off earlier when I'd said that we could still have fun in Paris without a party. She knew that my sensible head just needed further alcoholic persuasion to convince me of the right thing to do.

'Let's see what outfits we've got. I can sense a shopping spree coming on,' said Emma, disappearing to her room. 'Whatever you wear, it needs to be eye-catching, mouth-watering and sassy whilst remaining… stylish, elegant and classy. A difficult combination. You don't wanna look overly tarty; but you still need to be a bit loose and slutty. Your red *fuck-me-heels* will do nicely.'

'Nah, he saw me in those in Paris. I do love them, though,' I said.

Her contradictory advice made good sense. Short and tight-fitting usually worked well. I dashed to my wardrobe and pulled out the highest pair of black strappy heels that I owned. Finding shoes was never a problem. There were hoards in my wardrobe, which would have adequately kitted out a boutique shop. The only issue with the selected shoes was my inability to walk in them.

They required the expertise of Paris Hilton looking like a sex kitten on a pair of stilts. Instead, I resembled a child having stolen her mum's high heels. Stiletto heels, the killer variety and without a platform, only made an appearance on rare occasions where I knew no real walking was necessary. But I loved owning glamorous shoes, unable to resist elegant and transformative objects of desire for my feet, even if only to delight in ogling them, more than wearing. I made my appearance, strutting through to the lounge.

'Jesus. You're gonna need some practice in those,' Emma said.

'Do you think? I'm not that bad, am I?' I said.

She didn't answer. 'Help me roll up the rug; we may as well get started. This calls for serious party preparations,' she said, getting down on her knees and beckoning me over.

'But you hardly ever wear heels,' I said.

'Exactly. I'm not the one trying to be a slutty sex slave on stilts. I use my natural assets,' she said, shaking her cleavage and making a face at me whilst bent over the rug. 'Anyway, I'll keep you company and squeeze my feet into your shoes. Not that I'm an ugly sister, but it'll be fun.'

After we'd shifted the sofa and rearranged the furniture, we carried in the long dress mirror from my bedroom to our lounge and set up the runway. The laminate floor of the Penthouse was perfect for practising model walks. The big mirror was great for posing. Emma borrowed a pair of my heels, and having spent most of her life in Docs, she was like a bandy-legged cowboy.

Madonna blared out of our music system. Strutting down our make-do catwalk to *Like a Virgin*, then *Papa Don't Preach*, in all manner of outfits, wiggling our hips, swaying our shoulders and trying to lift our knees high to imitate runway models, we tried to find our sexy. Pausing only to hunt through our wardrobes for costume changes, I remembered my tight-fitting little red dress with the tiniest spaghetti straps and a v shape cut-out that plunged down my chest. I raced to put it on.

'Hard candy,' Emma shouted over the music as I twirled around. 'You look great in that. I think that's the one. You can just prop yourself up by a wall and look amazing. A proper *bum-tit*. He can't not notice you in that.'

'I think just turning up will get us noticed,' I laughed.

As I looked at my reflection, the dress hugged my figure in all the right places, giving me a pleasing silhouette. The pair of sheer tights helped hold my tummy in a bit firmer. I turned to check myself out from different angles and adjusted my posture by pulling myself upright and standing tall in the seductive black five-inch shoes. The shoes accentuated my chest and bum, like Emma had said. Outfit sorted, I slung my large case on the bed, ready to pack.

'You still need just a tiny bit more practice in those heels, though,' Emma added.

'Yeah, you're probably right,' I said.

In the mirror, I looked fine in a fixed pose. The issue was when I tried to walk. I'd got used to wearing a mid-heel court shoe most days and was a little stiff wearing the killer heel variety.

'I'm totally right if you're planning to wear them to try and impress Mr French,' she said.

'Better get practising then. They look so fancy and seductive, but they're such evil items of foot-burning torture,' I said, staring down at my feet.

It was early one morning. The buzzer rang. I was up and wearing my heels about the Penthouse and about to get ready for a mid-morning flight. I knew it was the milkman; no one else called so early.

The only reason we had a milkman was after Emma had spotted the athletic milkman that delivered down the road. He had biceps and a firm-looking arse. So, she'd called the company to get him to deliver to us, which had upped our grocery bill, but I'd fully supported her. I hadn't wanted to stand in the way between Emma and her eye candy. But when he'd first called at our door, on closer inspection, she'd found he wasn't that amazing. He was much older in the face than she'd realised. We both knew he'd been a disappointment to her, but neither of us had got around to cancelling him yet. He'd come to collect payment.

As I stood at the door, wearing my fluffy pink dressing gown, it was clear that he was more accustomed to the slipper look. Giving me the once-up-and-down manoeuvre with his head, he repeated then focussed on my feet, as if his eyes had deceived him. Looking like a hooker had become my new fresh-out-of-bed look. But I was civilised enough to be wearing a dressing gown, even if it was mid-length.

'G'morning,' he said, as I handed him a note and he rattled around for change in his bag, strapped over a shoulder.

'Morning,' I replied, whilst leaning against the doorframe and holding out my hand for the change. Then the postman came as the milkman headed off. I smiled. He handed me a wad of post, including a large envelope. We didn't make eye contact; I'd already done that with the milkman. I took the post, said thanks and closed the door.

Wandering back up the stairs, I simultaneously checked through it all. The big one was addressed to me. Noticing the large logo in bright colours on the envelope, I recognised it immediately. Tearing it open, my heart was racing. Scanning the contents of the letter, I skimmed to the part which read: *Delighted to offer you a position.*

'Oh shit. I got it, I got it,' I shouted, running into Emma's room waving the letter in the air. She was awake and sitting up in bed.

'Got what?' Emma said, looking bemused.

'The airline job. I got the bloody job!'

'Woo. High five,' she shouted with delayed enthusiasm, following my prompt as her brain caught up.

Jumping into her bed, I threw my arms around Emma and manically hugged her. 'Aahhhh,' I screamed. 'I *fucking* did it. I can't believe it.'

Emma attempted a camaraderie scream too but having not properly woken up, sounded more like she was distressed than excited.

'Ha ha. That's great. We'll have to celebrate. Great timing. A Paris party is just the thing. At least now you can be as bad ass as you want. And I can help with that.'

Returning to Paris

Sunday 24th August 2003

'Paris, here we come,' I said to Emma as we boarded the plane.

'Take two,' Emma added.

I shoved our duty-free bags into the overhead lockers, including the purchase of a last-minute bottle of *Glenfiddich*, remembering that he liked whisky. I had no idea about brands of whisky, but having seen older men opt for it on flights, I figured it suited the mature man. Emma bought some perfume that was on sale after having tested (on both of us) what smelled like most of the bottles on show. We were pungent.

I handed a distraction to Emma in the form of a copy of *Glamour* magazine – it had worked last time to dispel the nerves of flying, and although not her regular read, she'd been glued.

Across the Channel, we disembarked into the heat of the morning sun, taking us both by surprise.

'Bloody hell, it's hot.' Emma fanned her magazine in front of her face as she puffed out air from her cheeks.

The weather hadn't featured in my contingency plan. Kitted out for the chilly climate and rain that we'd left behind in unpredictable England, we were baking. I'd packed jeans and dark, heavy trousers and soon realised I was going to suffer mercilessly in the heat. We had our, or rather *my* party clothes, which had been the complete focus. Emma had helped herself to the contents of my wardrobe and added a few choice items that she'd selected, based on *bijou* and *chic* sophistication (her words), such as her charity shop beads, colourful scarf and fishnets. But we always shared, except I rarely did the borrowing. She'd also opted for my black prom style dress with frills that she'd selected during our dress-up session. Her choice was based entirely on the layers of fabric having wafted upwards when she'd spun around fast, which had satisfied a naughtiness in being able to show off her knickers if she wanted. On a regular day, she managed to incorporate black fishnet tights into her gothic look with DMs and somehow it suited her. She said a more glamourous affair was necessary for Paris, so she'd swapped the DMs for a pair of my black kitten heels, which she thought were *ooh la la* – a phrase I'd become accustomed to hearing too often. We were all set.

After collecting our bags and navigating the confusion of CDG Airport, we made it out of the terminal and luckily spotted a sign for the bus to the hotel. After a ten-minute wait of uncertainty, a minibus pulled up, displaying the name *Hotel Iris* on the side. We got ourselves on, found vacant seats and after a short drive we arrived at our Parisian destination. We weren't expecting much, just a base to dump our stuff and get ready, although our first impressions from the window of the bus pleasantly surprised us. The rate had included bed and breakfast, which had been a swaying factor in the selection criteria.

'Well, it's not The Ritz, but it doesn't look too bad,' I said.

'High praise coming from you,' said Emma.

'Well, we've only paid for three-star accommodation,' I reminded her.

Emma raised both thumbs before marching through the swing doors to the reception desk. After checking in, we were handed a large key on an even larger keyring of plastic. Leaving the reception area and trotting off to find our room, we soon discovered the charade. Once past reception, the grim reality of a three-star Parisian hotel lurked prominently.

'Blimey, it's like a prison block. Not that I've ever been banged up but if I was, this is how I'd expect it to be,' said Emma as she glanced at me with a smirk on her face.

'Yeah, 'cos they put you up in three-star hotels just like this,' I said.

Emma's observations were completely accurate.

'It stinks,' I said to Emma, wafting a hand to try and dispel the stench in the air.

She nodded in agreement as a smile crept over her face. It was dark, dank and dull, like a murky scene from a crime drama with a musty smell – possibly the smell of death. We wouldn't have known. Perhaps the corpse of a rat was rotting away up a drainpipe. There were chunks of plaster missing from the walls. It wasn't just in desperate need of a coat of paint, more like a complete refit. The patchy, threadbare yet stained carpet had seen better days. A prison may well have been more upmarket. I put the key in the lock and pushed down on the handle to reveal our room. It was poky.

'Perfect,' said Emma, barging past. 'It's the poshest hotel I've ever stayed in, in Paris.'

'It's the only Parisian hotel you've ever stayed in,' I said.

'Exactly,' she replied, laughing. 'It's got a decent-sized bathroom. There's a gap between the toilet and shower cubicle but you could use it as an all-in-one. No cheap frills like soap, though.'

'Doesn't matter. I've got shower gel and we only need a base,' I reminded her. 'We're getting our share of thrills being in the city of romance on a scorcher of a hot day with plans for party central. We just have to head out there into the action.'

She claimed the bed by the little window where the barely there, see-through curtains hung down. She dumped her case beside the bed and jumped on. She sprawled out, hands behind her head, then sat up quickly. 'You don't think we'll catch anything off the bed sheets, do you?' She smirked, trying to goad a reaction.

'Relax. Nothing more than crabs and bed bugs. You've probably caught worse in your lifetime,' I said. She grabbed a pillow and hurled it across at me.

'Bitch,' she shouted.

'Fucking bitch,' I replied. 'You've probably just scattered a few critters around doing that.'

'Good. Now let's get the bus into Paris,' Emma said.

Despite being willing to stay overnight, we both wanted to escape the hellhole of an excuse for a hotel. Our time was limited to two days for a leisurely adventure. Our holiday activities list included Emma wanting to see the Eiffel Tower and cruise down the Seine. Priority number one was buying booze for the party. Even though I'd bought a bottle of Glenfiddich as a gift, I felt we needed another gesture. Alcohol was a prerequisite to showing up unannounced. And an intentional last-minute email meant it was unlikely he'd be expecting us.

We boarded a coach from the hotel. I managed to negotiate two tickets for the centre of Paris, stopping at the Champs Elysees. We hadn't bargained on loads of other stops beforehand, totalling a forty-minute journey. But we treated it like a mystery bus tour special, like the ones advertised in travel agency windows. And the type of thing my gran used to love telling me about – a senior pensioner crowd on a day trip and the mystery being that the end destination is unknown; the difference being for us that we weren't pensioners and we knew where we were headed. Marc had taken me there a few weeks earlier. But we had no idea of the route, so we watched everything from the window, soaking it all up. After the pick-ups at the other hotels (most more upmarket than ours), a lot of it was just fast roads until I began to recognise landmarks, the obvious one being the Eiffel Tower. Then I remembered the roads making up that crazy star thing Marc had mentioned, and I knew we were there. The sun was blazing as we climbed off the bus, gagging for a drink.

'Remember the name of this road,' I said, looking up and pointing to the street sign. '*Avenue Carnot*. It's a long walk back to our hotel if we don't.'

Neither of us had a pen and we weren't particularly great with directions. Emma looked up at the sign. 'Avenue Car... not. That's easy. Let's rename it Carrot Avenue. We're bound not to forget that,' she laughed.

'Inspirational. Carrot Avenue it is,' I said.

Sometimes Emma had a spark. It wasn't genius, but she could be quick-thinking with a wicked sense of humour. Then there were other times when I wondered how she'd ever managed to become a librarian.

Still parched, we needed to grab a drink. We discovered café culture, although usually vibrant in Paris, to have greatly reduced options on a Sunday afternoon. We trundled down the street. A few more streets later, having got slightly lost, we consulted our map.

'We can't be that stupid. It's a bloody great big landmark,' said Emma, as she twisted the map around.

'Yes, we can. Let's not tell anyone about this,' I said.

We'd misinterpreted the map from the start, having mistakenly headed away from the centre, the big clue being the Eiffel Tower.

'Put it down to dehydration. I'm gasping,' Emma said, as she grabbed her throat and wiped her forehead, drama queen style.

We spotted a café / bar type place on a corner and made straight for it. Everyone else close by had had the same idea. The only tables left were those without parasols in direct hot sunshine. But with little choice, it had to do. Drinks first, comfort second.

'Can you get me some water?' asked Emma.

'Well, I would if I could remember the word for it in French. Can you have orange juice instead? I can do that,' I said.

My language skills were on a par with the equivalent of poor to zero. I pondered whether perhaps I should have taken my French dictionary and a pen.

'But I really want water. Well, they're bound to speak English, aren't they?' she said.

'Yeah,' I nodded.

Inconveniently, we discovered that the waiter only spoke French.

'Typical. We get the one that doesn't speak English. He probably doesn't like us because he'd rather be in his back garden chilling out than dealing with customers,' said Emma.

'Orange juice it is then,' I replied. '*Un jus d'orange, sil vous plait.*'

We also ordered ham and cheese sandwiches because that was the only option on the menu that we were confident of one hundred per cent. Neither of us fancied frogs' legs or snails by way of an accident, so we opted for safe, ordering a simple sandwich. On further inspection of the menu, we worked out we could order water by asking for *Evian* and *Perrier* – good old brand names.

'It's *oh mineral*,' Emma said, in a *eureka* type moment. She started laughing at herself, realising how funny she sounded, and repeated it, raising both her hands higher in the air in a prayer type fashion. '*Oh mineralll* – praise be,' she said, bowing her head at the table. 'Well, that's easy enough. We just have to associate water with prayer.'

'Okay. So far, carrots and prayer. There's probably a job out there for people like us,' I said.

'Like us divvies that can't remember any French from school? I wouldn't give us a job,' she said.

The waiter reappeared and placed down two plates of sandwiches.

'I'll remember Carrot Avenue. You remember water.' I laughed. 'So what would you have done for a drink and sandwich if I hadn't ordered them?'

'I would have used the international pointy method of course. It worked well in Spain,' she said.

We giggled with mouths full of sandwich.

When it came to pay the bill, Emma offered to take our cash inside. Moments later, she hurriedly rushed out.

'Quick, let's go. Think some bloke thought I was propositioning him,' she said.

She took off at speed down the street. I almost ran to catch up.

'Wait. What's going on?' I asked.

'He was wearing a white shirt and I tried to give him money… he looked like he was a waiter. I couldn't understand what he was saying, but I kept trying to give him money. He just looked at me and laughed… until the real waiter came over and sorted it out – felt a bit of a plonker,' she said, looking at me with an expression of seriousness.

I stopped momentarily, crossing my legs to avoid wetting myself. Imagining the scene, I wished I'd seen it, but the thoughts were entertaining enough.

'You could have bagged yourself that Frenchman you were after for the price of an orange juice and a sandwich,' I teased her, aware of the increasing need to find a loo.

In the street, we came across what looked like a space-age machine with a sign saying *toilettes*. We just had to figure out how many centimes and which buttons to enable us to successfully wee in the street. We passed the test. After consulting the map again (properly this time), we headed off in the direction of the Eiffel Tower. The streets were largely quiet compared to the time Marc had shown me around. Even though it was a Sunday afternoon, for a capital city it was almost deserted.

'Next on the list – if you see a shop, we need to buy beer for the party,' I said.

'Gotta find one that's open first.'

Just before reaching the Eiffel Tower, we found a small off-licence selling alcohol. Knowing how hard it was to find somewhere open selling alcohol, we decided to buy what we needed and carry it around with us – a couple of six-pack bottles of lager and two small bottles of water. The bag was heavy. There wasn't much choice, and that was all we could manage to carry between us. Little did we realise how popular we'd become with our bottles of lager, visible through our plastic bags. The streets got less quiet as people approached us, pointing at our bags, asking if they could buy it. At least that's what we thought they said. We just shook our heads. Had we wanted, we could have had a little lager racket.

Stopping off at the ornamental fountains near to a bridge over the Seine, we came across crowds of people sunbathing, some topless and others dipping their feet in the water. This was why the rest of Paris was deserted; they were all congregated at this spot. There were even TV cameras about, which we walked past a couple of times, thinking we might end up on French TV. They were filming the crowds, we guessed, due to the extreme weather, although we didn't really know, or care. We stopped for a break on the grass by a fountain.

'I can't be arsed doing any tourist stuff now. I think we've seen all of Paris by foot,' said Emma, wiping sweat from her brow.

'I'm so pleased you said that. Let's chill out here.'

I dumped the bags on the grass and sat on the floor. We rolled up our jeans and both of us stripped down our top halves without going fully continental – stopping at vest tops. I kicked water at Emma. Before long, paddling and splashing in the fountains ended in a full-on water fight. Getting soaked felt good as the cool water trickled down my skin, providing relief from the sun. Afterwards, we sat and looked longingly at our lager, both tempted to break it open. We resisted, probably only because we both knew we'd struggle to open it.

'You getting nervous about tonight yet?' Emma asked.

'Yeah, course. I've been nervous for the past couple of weeks with this and the interview,' I replied as I turned to speak to Emma, sheltering my eyes from the sun. 'But it's exciting at the same time, isn't it?'

'Definitely. Mr Paris just doesn't know what's in store for him. Will you tell him? About getting the job, I mean?' she said.

'Nah. What's the point? It won't make a difference. Do you think he'll mind us showing up?' I asked.

'I think he'll be mighty shocked. To turn up at his party without him expecting it, unless he's read his emails, and coming all the way over from England. He might wonder what you're up to. Then when he calms down, I'm sure it will be a big boost to his ego,' she said.

'I'm not doing it to boost his ego. I don't really know why I'm doing it anymore,' I replied.

'It's just a bit of fun… you mad, weirdo, STALKER WOMAN!' she shouted through cupped hands, attracting the attention of onlookers.

I pelted my shoe at her. She lobbed it back clumsily, and it landed in the fountain. She covered her mouth apologetically, but not so much that she offered to get it. It didn't matter; we were already drenched.

'Tell you what, let's do the river trip,' I said, fishing out my wet shoe and attempting to put it on. 'We can catch the breeze and dry out and you can look at the Eiffel Tower from the boat.'

My soggy shoe squelched when I walked.

'Okay. Only because it's literally across the road and over the bridge to get down to the boat. Any further and you'd have to carry me,' she said.

'Or abandon you,' I replied.

We managed to join a *bateau* about to depart. Neither of us wanted to climb the Eiffel Tower. Anything other than trying to dry out my shoe by sitting with one leg raised on Emma's lap, causing my body to drape over hers, was too much effort.

'We probably look like lesbian lovers,' I said, laughing, 'although I think I'd have better taste.'

She turned her head towards mine and gave me a lips kiss, wrapping her arm over my shoulder just to confirm any suspicions of onlookers. I pushed her off and then wiped my mouth.

'You're mental,' I said, as I rubbed the remnants of saliva visible on my arm.

'Are we having a lovers' tiff then?' she asked.

'Behave yourself, bitch,' I said, then turned and smiled at her.

The cruise down the Seine was perfect. We listened idly to the commentary which peacefully washed over us as we took in the sights of the Louvre, the Eiffel Tower and Notre Dame amongst other landmarks. Our faces became accustomed to the cool breeze flowing past. By the end of the tour, we had made a pact to come back and do the other Parisian stuff in future.

'We'd better get back to Carrot Avenue. This weirdo and her strange sidekick have a party to get to,' I said, climbing onto the bank.

'Maybe I could be your lesbian lover just for tonight. We could pretend we're over for a threesome. That would really get his attention,' she giggled.

'I don't think we're going to have any problems getting his attention. Anyway, you're not my type,' I said and pushed her away.

'Just a thought. I'm still going to snog a Frenchman after coming all this way,' she said.

'You've more chance if you're not lesbian then,' I reminded her.

'Could be bi. Blokes love that,' she said. 'Girls are so soft and delicious, *and* they know what feels good.' I shot her a glance. 'Fine. Straight it is. Remember, you're the one missing out,' she laughed.

'I can cope with that. Now grab a handle,' I said, separating the carrier bag handles, attempting to share the weight.

We lugged the heavy contents between us, one handle each, and meandered back to Carrot Avenue to await the coach.

THE TAXI RIDE

From the window of the bar, Emma and I watched a taxi pull up outside. The concierge had arranged its arrival. But I had to attempt negotiating getting us to the party. We'd already finished our drinks about five minutes beforehand, having settled on a pint of beer each, to try and relax. We didn't dare order another just in case the journey took longer than expected. The last thing I needed was to arrive desperate for the loo. Emma pulled me to my feet.

'Yay. Le taxi is 'ere! Now come on. You know this is a good idea. We haven't come all this way to wimp out now,' Emma said.

Her excitement wasn't infectious. I felt sick contemplating what we were about to do. But she had a point. The trip was about the party. We couldn't bottle out, even if it didn't seem such a great idea. Any other option felt a better idea. If Emma had persuaded me to *sack it off* and head for a Parisian nightclub, I'd have gone with it. But she didn't. She continued to pull me outside. We stood before the driver.

'Monsieur,' I said in my best French accent, then handed him a piece of paper containing Marc's address.

'*S'il vous plait,*' I added. Unsure if it sufficed, I stood and waited for his reaction, praying that it wouldn't require further interaction. The note was written in block capitals. It left no doubt about the spelling. The other last thing I didn't need was trying to explain the address due to bad handwriting. It took a couple of seconds before he nodded. Relieved, we climbed in and set off for Marc's house.

'Here we come, Mr French. There's no way he's going to expect this. This is totally mental. I can't wait to see his face,' Emma said.

I didn't reply, other than laugh, triggered by the toxic mixture of giddiness and alcohol. It felt like the high of having taken drugs, except for the mild panic.

♡

Eventually, we pulled up on a street that looked vaguely familiar.

'Yay. Is this it?' Emma said, patting my knee.

'Oh my God. What are we doing?'

Emma turned to face me. 'Now shut up and get a grip. This is just a party. It's all fine,' she said sternly. 'He'll be a bit surprised then everything will be okay. Promise.' Then she added, 'If it all goes tits up, which it won't, you're leaving the airline anyway. You'll never see them again.'

'Merci,' I said to the driver as he turned to face me and pointed at the fare. I handed him a large note, to avoid the complication of working out change.

We got out of the taxi to the sound of loud music playing with a Caribbean vibe. The raised pavement where we stood was at a gradient above his place. It was like being on stage prior to a performance, with the noisy commotion of chatter and music. It was full of people outside, even though I hardly dared look.

'Just breathe… and remember to walk like a hooker in your heels,' she said. I pulled my shoulders back. In the confines of my private space in the Penthouse, it had been easy to become a red-hot she-devil. But now I felt more schoolgirl tottering in stupidly high shoes.

'*Shit*. There he is. *Fuck*, I think he's seen us,' I said.

'Well; good. My God; is that him? He's totally not your type. I'm surprised you went for him. Not sure about the shorts look either,' she said.

'I didn't, it was the other way around,' I said.

'Not anymore or you wouldn't be here,' she giggled.

'*Shit*. He's coming over,' I said to Emma. '*Shit, shit, shit*,' I whispered to myself under my breath. Marc raced towards me.

It was the first time I'd witnessed him doing anything at speed, other than flying a plane. He was wearing long, baggy beach style shorts. As he got closer, his eyes were bulging wide. Emma stood behind me.

'What are you doing 'ere?' he blurted out, glaring at me.

I detected the panic in his voice. He wasn't smiling. Facing me, he waited for a response.

'We've come to your party,' I shrugged French style, and suddenly feeling completely sober.

'You didn't tell me you were coming,' he said. His wide-eyed expression suggested he was still either concerned or suspicious, I couldn't decide.

'Yes, I did. I sent you an email,' I said.

'You did? Well, I didn't get it,' he replied.

'Oh, well,' I said, shrugging again, having adopted his French mannerism with maximum effect. 'We're here. Are you pleased to see me?' My own words surprised me. He looked directly into my eyes.

'Of course,' he said.

I looked down, away from his gaze.

'Here,' I said, thrusting the box of whisky into his hands, 'I got you this.'

He opened the box and looked inside, despite the prominent label.

'It's my favourite,' he said, as he lifted the neck of the bottle and looked up. 'Thank you,' he said with a smile.

Emma emerged forward with the carrier bag of beer and an overenthusiastic wave.

'Hello, I'm Emma,' she announced.

'Sorry. This is my friend Emma. Emma, meet Marc,' I said.

Marc offered her a handshake, which she only just managed whilst struggling with the awkwardness of holding the bag.

''Ere, let me 'elp you with that,' said Marc, relieving Emma of the bag.

'We got you some beer too,' I added. He parted the handles and peered inside at the contents.

'Thanks,' he said with a frown. Then he stared at me blankly. 'Sorry, I just hadn't expected...' he began, then broke off. 'It's really good to see you.' He smiled again and leaned towards me, kissing my cheeks. 'Come on. You'd better come join the party.'

We followed him down to his courtyard. Then he dashed inside, carrying the stuff we'd offloaded. Aware of being watched by onlookers, a sea of mainly unfamiliar faces caught my eyes as I looked around. I recognised a couple of French colleagues from a distance, but I didn't know them.

Marc reappeared with two glasses.

' 'Elp yourselves to more drinks inside,' he said, as he handed us each a flute.

' 'Ow are things?' he asked, looking me up and down.

'Fine, thanks.' I shrugged, feeling awkward at not really knowing what to say, but conscious of his eyes wandering over my dress.

'I'm sorry, I was a little surprised at seeing you. I 'adn't expected...' his voice trailed off. 'But you look,' he paused again as he studied my figure, 'you look amazin', Avril,' he smiled. Then Marc's name was called from across the other side by a guy stood amongst a male group. 'Excuse me a moment. You know a few people from the airline. I leave you two to... 'ave a chat,' he said, turning to me and pausing for a moment, without saying a word.

His big familiar lips parted as he smiled again. His lingering look sent a nervous thrill through my body. As he gently brushed past, I caught the smell of his familiar musky scent. I inhaled the air.

'That went well,' Emma said. 'Come on, let's down this and get another. Think you need it.'

'You reckon? At first, I thought he didn't want us here,' I said.

'Yeah. It was tense, probably wondering what the hell you were doing. But once he got over the shock, he chilled out fast,' she sniggered.

We knocked back the fizz then headed inside via the kitchen door where it was noticeably cooler. No one else was there. Everyone else was outside in the heat of the evening sun.

'Oh, look,' said Emma, pointing at a heap of baguettes stacked up in one corner of the room. 'We're all right if we get hungry.'

Delighted with her find, she lifted a couple, taking one in each hand, and started to juggle.

'Put them back, you idiot,' I said.

'Why? It's completely mental. What's he gonna do with all these baguettes?' She laughed. 'I've never seen so many baguettes in one place, apart from a bakery.'

She was right; it was all wine and dry baguettes. Surveying the room, there was no other food on offer.

'Do you think he just ran out of time and thought *sod it*, they can all have free-flowing booze, so he just shoved all the baguettes to one side?' she asked. 'Or maybe he plans to hand them out like kids' party bags – here you go, shove that up your jumper.' She spun around and pulled up her dress to demo before getting conveniently distracted. 'Champagne!' Emma spied the open bottle on the kitchen worktop surface. I hurriedly topped up her glass with a foam of bubbles. 'I'm LOVING this party,' she mouthed dramatically.

'Come on, let's go back outside,' I said, after taking a sip.

'No way. I want to have a look around now. Anyway, you don't know anyone so what's the rush to get back outside?'

'And what is it you want to look at exactly?' I asked.

'Let's go and have a nosey round upstairs. Come on,' she said.

Without hesitation, Emma had already headed through the kitchen to the foot of the stairs. As she made her way up, I tagged on behind. There was no stopping her once curiosity took hold, and she needed close supervision.

'So, this is the *toilette*,' she said, flinging open the door to the bathroom. Pretending to use the bidet, she let out a gasp. 'Bloody hell. Look at all that champagne,' she squealed, as she rested her glass on the bath and clapped her hands. The bath was loaded with bottles of champagne on ice. 'Close the door. You can leave me here, I'm sorted,' she said, whilst pretending to climb in. 'Oh my God. Look, it's our beer,' she pointed. '*Shit*. Next to the loo.'

'Still in the carrier bag,' I added.

'Well, I bloody hope he's not planning to piss it away down there. I'll take it home with me if so.'

'No, you bloody won't!' I told her. 'Anyway, why'd you want the cheap stuff when you've got all this champagne?' I asked.

'I don't like waste – not when it's booze. You made me go half way across Paris in the scorching heat to get it. But okay, I'll behave myself, but only 'cos you want me to act posh and sophisticated,' she said.

'Keep trying,' I teased.

'Slag. Bitch. Tart,' she retorted.

'Shhh, no one knows that,' I replied, laughing with a two-finger gesture.

Noticing a glass bottle of aftershave on the small shelf below the mirror, I picked it up. Holding it in my hand, first studying the silver label, then shaking the liquid and watching it settle through the dark glass, I removed the shiny gold top. Leaning over it, I delved in, taking a sniff of his aftershave like a line of cocaine. I breathed in his scent. The one he always wore. Earlier, I'd recognised it immediately when he'd stood close and then our bodies had touched. It was a good fix. I exhaled. Emma watched.

'We really need to get you some more champagne, don't we? Pity there's no bottle opener in here,' Emma said. 'But first, where's the bedroom?'

Obediently, without thought, I automatically pointed. She walked over and went straight in. Instantly, I regretted it.

'You can't just do that,' I said.

'Do what? I'm having a look at his shag pad,' she replied over her shoulder to me. 'The dirty den of demon deeds. I bet zis iz where all zee action takes place,' she said, in a lousy pretend accent.

'Weirdo. Why'd you need to look at his bedroom anyway?'

''Coz then I can picture all the dirty details you've told me,' she replied, with a filthy exaggerated laugh.

'You're such a crazy bitch,' I sighed.

Standing at the door, I peered inside. It was just an ordinary bedroom now, not a place of nervous anticipation like it had been, at first. On closer inspection, there were stacked-up boxes on one side. *So he is actually going*, I whispered to myself. Not that it was unexpected.

'*Shit*. Someone's coming,' I said to Emma. She smirked, then instantly covered her mouth, pretending to be serious. Footsteps on the stairs grew louder. 'Quickly,' I said, and rushed over to grab Emma's hand and yanked her onto the bed. We both listened to the sounds. The bathroom door slammed closed. 'Phew.'

'What were you planning to do with me on the bed?' Emma smiled.

'If anyone comes in, we just say you're feeling ill and so came to have a lie-down,' I said. Then I tiptoed over to the bedroom door and pushed it ajar, and my ear to the door. 'Shhh,' I said to Emma, signalling for her to lie back down.

As the toilet flushed, Emma obeyed, leaning back. The bathroom door lock opened. The footsteps disappeared back downstairs.

'No handwashing. That's got to be a man,' Emma said.

'Come on, let's go,' I said.

The potential embarrassment at being caught snooping in Marc's room was enough to feel total relief when we made it back downstairs.

'We've got to find me a Frenchman to snog,' Emma said, as I refilled a couple more glasses in the kitchen, having left the empties in the upstairs bathroom.

'So long as you don't make us look like a couple of cheap English tarts,' I said.

'Don't be so boring. Anyway, promise I won't do anything you've not done,' she laughed.

'Very funny.'

We went back outside amidst the groups of French chatter. It was preferable to be gawped at, rather than caught out like some obsessive stalker. Looking around, I spotted a young tanned man with a shaved head, sitting by himself.

'He's an outcast like us,' I said to Emma, as she followed my gaze.

'Excellent. Snog potential. Let's go make friends,' she said, and headed off in his direction. I let her go alone.

Watching Marc, he was still with the same group of guys from earlier. I couldn't stop myself staring. But on hearing Emma's voice, I turned away.

'Avril, come and meet Pedro,' she repeated. 'He's Spanish.' The novelty of calling me Avril was a source of amusement.

'Hello,' I said to Pedro, holding out my hand politely, which he shook.

He managed to say *hello* back. Then after a few general, getting-to-know-you type questions that didn't warrant much of an exchange between us, we soon discovered that his English was up to the same standard as our French, which was almost non-existent. But it didn't deter Emma from trying. The combination of fizz, relaxed music, overly slow exaggerated-mouthed-talking and a bit of *pointy method*, as Emma called it, and we found ourselves positioned on Pedro's knee, one leg each. Not that I cared or had any interest, unlike Emma. I was preoccupied, stealing glances at Marc. I wasn't entirely sure how the progression from a *hello* to a *knee sit* had occurred, or how Emma's hands had become busy, buffing up Pedro's bald-looking head like petting an expectant puppy. She kept mentioning how she couldn't work out who it was that he knew at the party. I couldn't care less. No one except Emma was paying him any attention, until I joined in for entertainment. As I knocked back Marc's champagne, the alcohol fuzzed my brain. Every now and then, I'd burst into a bizarre fit of giggles. The absurdity of rubbing the Spanish man's shaven head was both distracting and weirdly comforting.

'He keeps looking at you, you know,' Emma spouted.

'He's not coming over,' I said.

'You're in the lap of another guy… could be sort of awkward,' she said.

'No. He doesn't want me.'

'You don't know that. Here, hold this, I'm taking Pedro for a dance,' she said, whilst giving me her glass after climbing off his knee. Then she grabbed Pedro by the hands, pulling him to his feet.

I downed the champagne. Then I consoled myself further by starting on the remains of hers, before walking over to the stone wall to rest the empties. There'd been little more than stilted conversation and a few glances. *But what did I expect?* I asked myself.

'There you are,' Marc said, from over my shoulder. I almost froze. 'You did send me an email. I got it.'

'Oh good. So, it's all okay then?' I asked. The words came tripping out of my mouth before I could stop myself unintentionally seeking his permission and sounding very uncool.

'Of course. I'm sorry I didn't get in touch, but we spoke about…'

I replied, almost apologetically for him.

'It's okay. I understand. I hoped you wouldn't mind me coming; it was a last-minute thing…'

My mouth was incapable of speaking the truth. *Who makes a last-minute decision to attend a party in another country?* The close proximity of him made it barely possible to look him in the eyes.

''Ere,' he said, 'let me fill it for you.'

He stood so close. The air was filled with his scent, enveloping me. I could feel his breath on my face, sending a tingle of nerves through me as he spoke. Haphazardly, I reached for my glass. His arm outstretched, he brushed my hand with his. As a quiver of shockwaves passed through me, I relinquished my grasp. Fleetingly, our eyes met. Then he stood back. I forced myself to resist an urge. Taking a breath, the moment passed.

He re-emerged with more champagne. 'You know, I'll be leaving in a couple of weeks. I'm packing right now.'

'Yes, I saw…' I stopped myself. He mustn't find out I'd been snooping around his bedroom. 'Things look different and you said you'd be going,' I replied, trying to act blasé.

'Yes. I am. I'm only sorry that…' he said.

He turned to face me, grabbed my hand and pulled me inside the porch. Bewildered by his actions, the touch of his hand, so familiar yet unexpected, I stood back. He placed his arm around my waist and pulled me towards him. His body on mine. Then he released his grip as quickly as he'd drawn me near. Someone was coming down the stairs.

'Marc.' A voice interrupted. 'You didn't tell me that April was coming.'

It was Pierre from the airline. He greeted Marc with a friendly slap on the back and a grin in my direction. We'd worked together a few times. He was cabin crew too but much older. The grey flecks of hair around his temples suggested he was in his forties. He leaned in to me, still grinning. The fumigating booze on his breath was pungent; I averted my head to avoid the stench.

'Who'z your friend?' he enquired. His eyes flashed with interest.

I looked at Marc. One of us had to get rid of Pierre. Politely, I took Pierre by the arm as we went outside to meet Emma. She could handle both him and Pedro, just for a bit. Then I dashed back inside, almost breaking into a run were it not for the heels. Stepping into the porch and expecting to find Marc, he'd gone. My shoulders slumped with disappointment. 'Damn, why couldn't he have just waited?' I said out loud. *Was he intentionally tormenting me?* I looked around for him inside, but his disappearance convinced me that he wasn't bothered.

In the courtyard, Emma was locked in a snog with Pierre. I shouldn't have left her alone. It was a record time even for her. Having known him less than five minutes, it wasn't a joke. She'd wanted to kiss a Frenchman. Any Frenchman, it seemed. Even one that reeked, although she probably did too. *And what did it matter? And who cared what anyone thought?* We didn't know them, any of them... much. The alcohol had numbed any irritation of cringeworthy behaviour. I threw back my head and laughed.

A while later, post-lip lock, Pierre was busy trying to get Emma's number, handing her a pen and paper, which she kept drawing smiley faces on. He was out of luck. Pierre was just a lip-dance at a Parisian party. I knew that. Emma didn't want a romance, just a frog to snog. I almost felt sorry for him.

'Avril. Can we talk?' Marc had taken hold of my hand, before I registered his voice. I nodded in surprise to see him standing in front of me again. I assumed he must have witnessed the whole scene with both of our mates, resulting in his swift attention. He led me back to the porch. Only this time he closed the door.

'Sorry about Emma,' I began.

'Sorry it's taken me so long to be able to talk to you. And then what 'appened earlier. This may be unfair to say it, but I've not stopped thinking about you. I really wanted to see you,' he said.

I pulled his face to mine without hesitation and snogged him greedily. The feel of his big soft lips reminded me how I'd missed him. How I wanted him. Forcefully, as I pressed up against him, he lifted me to him. Instinctively, I wrapped my legs around him. The smell of him, the touch of his skin and the feel of his hair as my fingers grasped him were all so familiar. Starving for him, my hand reached down for the hard bulge in his trousers. Then withdrawing his lips and pulling away, he let out a sigh and put me down.

'We can't,' he said, closing his eyes momentarily and rubbing his face with his hands.

'But…' I began.

'Of course, I want you. More than that even. Look at me, the state I'm in.' He gaped down at his trousers to where my hand had rested moments earlier. 'But it would make things worse. Nothing 'as changed, Avril. I'm still leaving.' He shrugged.

'I thought you were about to tell me something,' I said.

'Yes, to talk to you. To see 'ow you are. I'm suffering with you being 'ere like this,' he said, pulling his hands through his hair and readjusting himself. 'Seeing you flirting with that guy over there, I was so jealous. I 'ate 'im. The thought of you with someone else. But that is selfish of me.'

'I'm not interested in *him*…' I said.

'Let's not do this again. It was bad enough the first time. You know 'ow I feel. There, I've said it.' His eyes gazed directly at mine.

'But it's not enough,' I said.

'It's circumstances… you know that,' he replied.

He was right. But I couldn't prevent the feeling of being torn apart inside. He took hold of me and wrapped his arms comfortingly around my shoulders, stroking and kissing my hair. I had to pull away. I unlocked myself from his embrace. Defiantly, I wiped away a tear.

'I'm so sorry. I wish things were different,' he said.

'Think it's best I go now,' I replied, biting my lip.

''Ow are you getting to your 'otel?' he asked.

'I've got the number of a taxi to call,' I replied.

'That's not gonna work,' he said, raising both his eyebrows. His expression changed to a look of genuine concern. 'You don't understand. Taxis don't work the same way 'ere as they do in the UK. If they don't want to come out at night, then they won't. And it's past midnight now.' He shrugged. 'Wait 'ere. I'll sort you a lift out.' Then he walked off, leaving me to pretend I was okay. I flicked my wrist over my cheeks and wiped underneath each eye with a finger to remove any smudged liner. If I told myself I was okay, then perhaps I could convince myself.

Outside, I saw Marc speaking to Pierre. It was all sorted in a matter of moments. Pierre was all grins when he made his approach to tell me he was only too pleased to help take us back to our hotel.

'*Shit,* that was never the plan,' mumbled Emma, just audible enough for me to hear.

I managed a strained wave to Marc and swiftly departed with Emma, purposefully avoiding saying goodbye. I couldn't trust myself not to blurt out something completely ridiculous if we'd spoken. He didn't attempt to stop me. It was best that way. I knew there'd never be a tinge of regret on my part.

♡

The morning after, I awoke as the sunlight filled our room. There were no blackout curtains afforded to our hotel. The sun highlighted the shabbiness of everything about the room. My memory was on catch-up, so far remembering that I'd crashed into bed fully clothed, minus my shoes. Emma was still fast asleep and semi-conscious on the bed, lying flat out, also fully clothed in last night's outfit. Her mouth was open, and a rumble of snores escaped periodically and compounded how odd she appeared. I laughed. Distracted by needing to pee, I held on, trying to squeeze my pelvic floor tight, which I only managed when I clenched my teeth. I didn't want to pass up the opportunity of a golden moment and lifted the camera from its case. Trying to stifle my laughter and avoid waking her or wetting myself, aware of how desperate the need had become, camera in hand, I tilted forward. Positioned over the top of her head, finding the best angle, I zoomed in and snapped comedy gold. Her eyes blared open.

'You… bitch,' she croaked, like an old witch, squinting her eyes partly open. In slow motion, she raised her middle finger at me.

I let out a roar of laughter then rushed to the loo, trying not to completely piss myself on the way and already alarmed by the trickle that had escaped.

'Good morning, gorgeous,' I shouted from the loo.

'What time's it?' she grunted.

'Too early, but we may as well get up now you're awake,' I shouted again from the bathroom.

'I'm still in my clothes,' she said, as I re-emerged from the toilet.

'Me too.'

I passed her a glass of water.

'Last night, I didn't do anything bad, did I?' Emma said.

'What; like the stuff you did to that Frenchman?' I asked. 'I reckon he thought his lucky day had finally arrived. Anyway, you weren't paralytically drunk, just bladdered enough.' Emma never suffered from convenient *forgettery* of the night before. She was just seeking approval for her actions. 'I think we'll remember this for quite a long time,' I said.

'Good. That's okay then. I'm starving. Shall we see whether the breakfast in this place is edible?' she replied.

Breakfast was a continental affair, which was a relief as everything came in packets. I'm not sure we would have risked it otherwise. We had some standards.

As we chatted over breakfast, every now and then one of us would giggle, remembering something from the night before.

'Do you remember the look on his face when we turned up?' Emma said.

'His eyes practically jumped out of his head. He totally hadn't expected us to show up,' I said.

'I actually felt a bit sick for you when we arrived in that taxi, but I didn't want to say.' Emma giggled.

'Imagine how I felt,' I replied.

'You've got balls, I'll give you that,' Emma said, in between shovelling in heaped spoonfuls of cereal. 'It was crazy, but brilliant.'

'No, just stupid,' I replied.

'What were we doing to that Spanish man?' Emma asked.

'You mean, what were you doing? You started it. Anyway, who cares? He seemed to enjoy himself,' I said.

'Yeah. He probably got jealous when I ditched him for a slice of Pierre,' she said.

'Do you think Marc will think about me?' I asked.

'I doubt he'll ever forget you after that stunt,' she replied.

Despite feeling slight heartache, I smiled inwardly, knowing there'd be no one as foolish as me that he'd likely remember more.

'Ha ha. It was fun, wasn't it?' I said.

'Yeah. Now we need to find us another party to go to,' she said.

'We might struggle, unless you hit it off with Pierre,' I replied.

'Oh my God.' Emma put her hands over her face. 'I just remembered that I gave him my number.'

'No,' I said in disbelief, recalling the smiley faces I'd seen her draw.

'Well, he just kept trying so hard,' she said.

'What, like a pest?' I asked.

'A bit, I suppose. Yeah. But a nice one,' she laughed.

'You callous cow. He'll think he's got a chance now,' I laughed.

'Don't remind me. If he calls, I just won't answer. Kindest way,' she said. 'What time we gettin' back?'

'Midday. We'll pack and head out after this.'

♡

We checked out of our prison block and caught the bus back to the airport, both of us still buzzing from alcohol. On the bus, the motion made me doze in a contented slumber. But as it jerked over bumps or abruptly turned corners, it caused my head to occasionally smack the window and my eyes to flash open. Emma laughed, every time.

THE FINAL CHAPTER

Marc had been a taste of something different. And having tried just a sample, I wanted more. He'd introduced me to a world away from my own, and all the ingredients had combined to produce a recipe for a high-octane and addictive adventure.

He was an obsession for a while – the route of my addiction, and the darker side of love. When I allowed my mind to wander, he invaded my thoughts… hearing his soft French accent, picturing his tanned body and sensing his tender touch. And unable to let go altogether, even though we were miles apart, I kept him with me in my dreams, closing my eyes to be with him.

Even months later, occasionally, he stirred my mind – a mention of Paris on the news, and when the French café opened in town, and when I gazed up at a plane flying overhead on a sunny day. Sometimes, I'd smile and whisper a quick *hello* to my pilot in passing as he glided across the sky at around six hundred miles per hour. He'd always occupy a little tucked-away corner of my heart, the place reserved for fond memories.

Those feelings were never lost. But over time, they got shelved. Hidden away like forgotten items stored in a dusty cardboard box.

♡

One evening, during a wardrobe clear-out, I'd been tugging at some clothes. A folder fell, bumped me on the head and landed on the floor. It was a diary and scribbled notes. I took it as a sign. Four years later, I completed my novel.

At the time, I promised myself that if it got published then I'd tell him. Like a poetic justice to the past. He was my inspiration. But as my fingers had tangoed with the keyboard, I'd wondered whether to leave the past alone. Eventually, I gave in to temptation with a few clicks on Instagram. And there he was.

He looked a bit *George Clooney-esque*, sat on a sailing boat. He'd grown a beard and wore mirrored sunglasses. I trawled his stories and brought his past into my present. The *what if* scenario played out in my head, wondering. And I let him intimidate me again. In a weak-at-the-knees kind of way, picturing myself on his boat. Two sunset lovers sailing the sea on calm waters. I giggled at the thought. And bet his boat doubled as a love palace, although in my mind he remained a free spirit in the sky and a prize fish swimming in the ocean, rather than working on his count of reef knots.

Then I wrote to tell him. I reminded him that he'd promised to buy it. But I didn't really expect a reply. Years had passed, and I doubted he'd remember me.

Days went by. But when Marc's name popped up on my screen, a shot of adrenalin rushed through my body. He apologised for the delay, saying he'd been at sea. And he told me about living in Germany, where he'd been for almost fifteen years. After that, we corresponded for a few weeks.

He never took the job in Indonesia. He became a captain at a German airline. At the time, he'd tried contacting me by email to let me know. But he never heard back. When I asked why he hadn't tried my mobile, he'd assumed that I'd moved on with my life. And I had, but not in the way he thought.

After getting the long-haul job and with Emma's promotion, we upgraded our address to an apartment with modern technology and broadband. We got new internet-based email addresses and let our old technology lapse. Neither of us got many emails back then.

Today

I'm holding in my hand a copy of my novel, *Lost in Bittersweet Clouds*. The inscription inside my book reads: *To Marc, wherever you are in the world…*

And about to board a plane for Paris, a half-way meeting point for old times' sake, I have just as many butterflies as that girl in her twenties.

I hope he likes it.